D1084126

Lost Cove

by

George Spain

Based on *Lost Cove,*
the Unpublished Autobiography

of

Jeremiah Vann

Published by Westview, Inc.
Kingston Springs, Tennessee

ISBN 978-1-62880-010-4

Published by Westview, Inc.
P.O. Box 605
Kingston Springs, TN 37082
www.ideasintobooks.net

Printed in the United States of America on acid free paper.

Also by George Spain

Our People: Stories of the South
Delightful Suthun Madness XIII

For Jackie

Table of Contents

Acknowledgments

Early on, my mother taught me to love books and I have ever since. From my parents and grandparents, and from Jackie's family, have come many of the stories I tell. I owe much to them.

During all of my many years of scribbling on paper there have been people who kindly read the words, or listened to me read them. Some said, "I like your writing!" What more does a writer need to keep going than to have the support and suggestions of Jackie, Trina (Spain) Flynn, Adam, Brad, Lynch and Darwin Spain; Mary and George Brazil; Nick Boone; Carolyn Wilson; Maxine and Harry Rose; Jane Myers, Sandy Zeigler; Elizabeth and Emmitt Logsdon; and Mary Elizabeth Nelson.

Special acknowledgments go to Sally Lee, Louise Colln, and Gayle and Jerry Henderson who were invaluable in reading the complete manuscript and helping in editing, proof reading and sharing their knowledge and experience toward this project.

Even though I was a boy when it all happened, and even though I loved my mother dearly, there was a long time in my life when I believed what she had done with Captain Taggert was wrong, and that she was partly to blame for his death – but as I grew older and committed my own sins I began to think, who am I to stand in judgment of my mother who had loved me and cared for me without anyone's help, and who am I to judge anyone, even the Taggerts, for I have done terrible things in my life: I've been a drunkard and been lascivious, and I have cursed God, and I've killed three people – so who am I to judge anyone?

Jeremiah Vann
October 1944

Prologue

In the summer of 1945, Levi Thomas Crowley was buried beside the empty graves of his parents in Lost Cove, two miles south of Sewanee, Tennessee. The next morning his wife, Lillie Jane, dragged his sea chest out into the back yard, poured kerosene over it and set it on fire. Had their daughter, Fannie, not seen the chest burning and put the flames out, no one would have ever known who Levi Thomas Crowley really was.

Years later, Fannie told me what happened that day but she never explained why her mother had tried to destroy the chest or what had happened to it. She never spoke of it again. She died in Nashville in 1992.

Fannie Crossley Spain was my mother. Levi Thomas Crossley was my grandfather. He and my grandmother once owned Lost Cove.

Four weeks after my mother died in Nashville, my two sisters and I began to get her house and furniture ready for an estate sale. Late on the second evening, they went home and left me working alone in the attic. I was tired and about ready to leave when I moved four large cardboard boxes of Christmas decorations. There, behind them in the corner, was an old chest. I pulled it into the middle of the floor and kneeled down in front of it.

It was battered and worn. Its dark-stained wood was bound around with three bands of black iron. Patches of wood were glued and nailed over cracks. The lid and one side were blackened and slightly charred. I wondered: *Is this the chest?* The key was in the lock; my hand shook as I turned it. At first it wouldn't move, then I tried again, this time more carefully. It clicked open. The hinges made a raspy screech as I raised the lid.

Immediately, a musty odor filled the air. Inside was a jumbled stack of old books. I took them out, one at a time. Penciled in the center of the inner cover of each book was, "Jeremiah Vann". The name, I assumed, was that of the original owner from whom my grandfather had bought them. Most were over a hundred years old. There were outdated works on history, geography, ocean-ography, agriculture, the disease and treatment of farm animals, religion, philosophy, and Greek and Latin lexicons. I thought: *If this old stuff was in his sea chest, maybe my grandmother had just wanted to get rid of some worthless junk.*

I was disappointed in what was there. But just as I was about to close the lid, I picked up a large 1918 World Almanac. Beneath it, wrapped in wax paper, was a dried leather satchel with a U.S. Army insignia. The leather cracked as I unbuckled the strap and pulled out a yellowed 1864 newspaper, the *Nashville Dispatch.* Also in it were two wooden boxes: the smaller one contained a ring and comb carved from bone, the larger held a matched pair of Colt pistols. There was no explanation as to whom these had belonged. Beside the box was a leather-covered Bible, in the front of which was a long lock of rust-red hair tied with a black ribbon and in the back an envelope and letter signed by Lucy Taggert. On the first three pages of the Bible were three names written in different handwriting: "Father Patrick McGrath," "Annie Lynch" and "Katherine Lynch O'Connor", names I had never heard. Near the back, a single page had been torn out. Underneath the box was a gray cloth-covered book, with dark green leather on its corners and spine. I lifted it out, turned to the second page and read aloud, "Lost Cove Dedicated to my precious Lillie Jane who saved me from Hell. What is written here is for our people after I am gone. Jeremiah Vann, Lost Cove, August 1944." I read it again. As I did, questions arose in my mind: *Who was Jeremiah Vann and why did he name the title of his book after my grandparents' place? Who were the two women whose names were written in the Bible? Was the dedication to 'Lillie Jane' to my grandmother or someone else? Why had my grandfather hidden these things in the bottom of his sea chest and why had my mother hidden the chest in her attic? Was there something here that my grandparents and mother didn't want anyone to know about?*

I turned the page and began to read and did not stop until I finished it hours later. Tears were in my eyes as I closed the book. I was filled with pride and love for my grandparents, and for the story of our people; and for the mountains and valley that had fed, clothed and sheltered them for five generations. For one hundred and seventy years the valley had received them into its earth.

My God, what a senseless loss it was, when it was sold in 1954. Likely, our grandchildren will never set foot there nor see the beauty of this land that was once ours.

There is much cruelty and sadness in my grandfather's story but also much to be proud of. It is a story filled with love and it tells us—his descendants—who we are, where we came from and the truth about who he was.

As I read the last pages, I was a little boy again. I could see my grandfather clearly, sitting in front of his fireplace, writing in the very book I was holding in my hands, occasionally looking up to stare into the flickering flames, stroking his large white mustache, relighting his corncob pipe, the smoke curling above his head.

I could feel myself sitting there on his lap, hearing his gentle voice in my ear, telling me about rounding Cape Horn where waves were higher than the masts of his ship, and I could see my fingers touching the faded blue anchor tattooed on his left forearm, and I could smell the rich smoke rising from his pipe. O, how I loved him.

The Manuscript

I have worked on and off on my grandfather's story for ten years, making corrections that will help the reader concentrate on the content while retaining my grandfather's voice, so that it accurately portrays his extraordinary life and times and the beauty of his valley, Lost Cove.

Jeremiah Vann wrote *Lost Cove* in a fine-quality maritime logbook that measures nine by fourteen inches. In it are three hundred cream-tinted pages with light green lines. Twelve pages have been torn out. The outer edges of the paper are slightly yellowed. The jacket is covered in dove gray cloth; the corners and spine are dark green leather. The binding is still tight.

Except for five pages in black ink, the writing is all in pencil. Apparently his hand was shaky for some words and sections are hard to read and others have been smudged by erasures and written over. A few places are splotched by dark brown stains.

The first entry was made in April 1942, the last in August 1944. Shifts in time sequences, from the past to his immediate worries and thoughts, are at times confusing and indicative of his mental decline. His erratic punctuation would have been distracting to the reader so it has been corrected. After sailing the seas of the world for many years he had developed a good ear for dialect, so the spelling of this remains as he wrote it. Rather than using chapter numbers he dated the sections as he wrote them, by the month and year. They vary considerably in length. His pattern was to write at least once a month. The headings of the six parts are mine.

Jeremiah Vann was seventy-eight when he began writing and eighty when he finished. During these two and a half years he realized his mind was deteriorating. His increasing confusion of memory and difficulty in maintaining the focus of his thoughts are apparent in the writing. Yet even with his age and the onset of his mental decline, the reader will still readily recognize he was a man of intelligence with a constant love for his family.

Two genealogical tables have been included at the beginning to help place individuals within their family relationships over the course of three centuries. There is also a copy of the 1974 Tennessee Valley Authority topographical map of Lost Cove and some of the surrounding area south of Sewanee. The map shows the Pearson/Vann house, Big Sink, the road to Sewanee, Natural Bridge, the Saddle, Prince Spring and the family cemetery, now called the Garner Cemetery; references are made to all of these in the manuscript.

At the end of the manuscript he pasted in part of the chapter on Franklin County in Goodspeed's *History of Tennessee,* published in 1887. It remains the best summarized history of the early years of Franklin County where the majority of the story takes place. I have put it in the back as Appendix I.

I added Appendix II, which includes extracts from *The Memoirs of Lieut. Henry Timberlake, (Who accompanied the Three Cherokee Indians to England in the year 1762),* first published in 1765. It gives a first-hand description of the Cherokee less than forty years before my great, great grandfather Levi Washington Pearson encountered them.

George Spain

The Vann Family

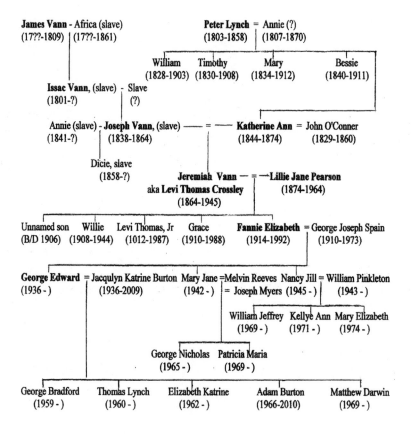

The Pearson Family

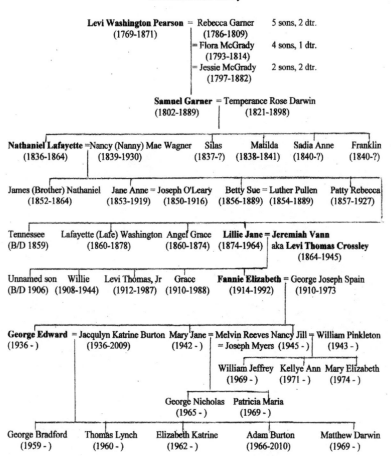

Levi Washington Pearson = Rebecca Garner   5 sons, 2 dtr.
(1769-1871)   (1786-1809)
= Flora McGrady   4 sons, 1 dtr.
(1793-1814)
= Jessie McGrady   2 sons, 2 dtr.
(1797-1882)

Samuel Garner = Temperance Rose Darwin
(1802-1889)   (1821-1898)

Nathaniel Lafayette =Nancy (Nanny) Mae Wagner   Silas   Matilda   Sadia Anne   Franklin
(1836-1864)   (1839-1930)   (1837-?)   (1838-1841)   (1840-?)   (1840-?)

James (Brother) Nathaniel   Jane Anne = Joseph O'Leary   Betty Sue = Luther Pullen   Patty Rebecca
(1852-1864)   (1853-1919)   (1850-1916)   (1856-1889)   (1854-1889)   (1857-1927)

Tennessee   Lafayette (Lafe) Washington   Angel Grace   **Lillie Jane** = **Jeremiah Vann**
(B/D 1859)   (1860-1878)   (1860-1874)   (1874-1964)   aka **Levi Thomas Crossley**
(1864-1945)

Unnamed son   Willie   Levi Thomas, Jr   Grace   **Fannie Elizabeth** = George Joseph Spain
(B/D 1906)   (1908-1944)   (1912-1987)   (1910-1988)   (1914-1992)   (1910-1973

George Edward = Jacqulyn Katrine Burton   Mary Jane = Melvin Reeves   Nancy Jill = William Pinkleton
(1936 -)   (1936-2009)   (1942 -)   = Joseph Myers (1945 -)   (1943 -)

William Jeffrey   Kellye Ann   Mary Elizabeth
(1969 -)   (1971 -)   (1974 -)

George Nicholas   Patricia Maria
(1965 -)   (1969 -)

George Bradford   Thomas Lynch   Elizabeth Katrine   Adam Burton   Matthew Darwin
(1959 -)   (1960 -)   (1962 -)   (1966-2010)   (1969 -)

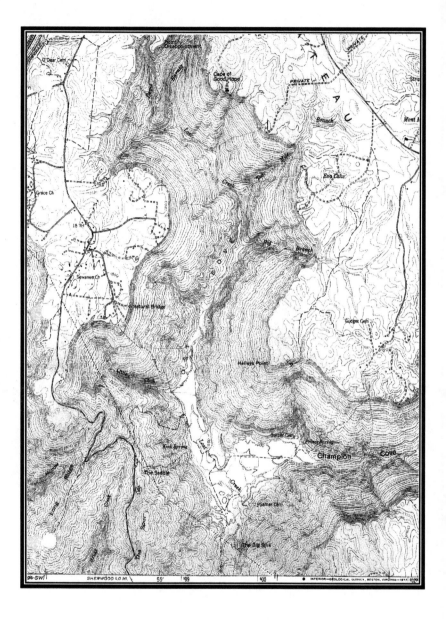

Lost Cove

by

Jeremiah Vann

Dedicated to my precious Lillie Jane
who saved me from hell. What
is written here is for our people after I am gone.

Jeremiah Vann
Lost Cove
August 1944

Part I

The Pearsons and the Vanns

April 1942

God, help me remember; my mind is slipping away.

I am writing in the library. Through the window, I see the pink sandstone obelisk that Lillie Jane's grandfather, Levi Washington Pearson, cut from the mountain and carved to God one hundred and sixty years ago. It is seven feet tall and two feet square at the base; the surface is pocked and splotched like old skin. Halfway up the side that faces north and the open fields, he carved, *"And the Lord appeared unto Abram, and said, Unto thy seed will I give this land: and there builded he an altar unto the Lord, who appeared unto him."* *Genesis 12:7.* It stands in the front yard among the beeches and beside the path that leads down to the spring and on to the wagon road that runs the length of the valley and up the mountain to Sewanee. In the evening of the day he finished the monument, he poured the blood of a calf over the obelisk and burned the calf's carcass before it.

A hard, cold, steady rain is falling. The low places have filled with water; the creek is almost out of its banks. Another day of this will fill the Big Sink and then Lost Cove, and Buggytop Cave will begin to flood and Crow Creek will be out of its banks all the way to Sherwood.

When I was nine, my mother told me that during the flood of 1860, a witch with long red hair floated across the Cove's muddy waters in a sky-blue eggshell and that John O'Connor, who probably would have been my father if he had not drowned, was swept into the Big

Sink—pieces of his body were later found in Buggytop Cave.

When the Cove floods the waters carry away topsoil and fences. Some of our hogs and calves will likely drown and Lillie Jane and I will be marooned here on the hill until the water goes down. The fields will be gullied and covered with brush and logs; it leaves a mess to clean up. Thank God old Levi picked this spot to build his house. When the fields dry, the surface is littered with remnants of my ancestors: pieces of stone images and tools, flint spear points and arrowheads and there will be bits of coral and fluted shells—tiny as a fingernail—and the bones of animals and humans.

The stone carvings were made by my great grandfather's people, the Cherokee, and the old ones before them. For hundreds of years they came to this cove staying only long enough to hunt buffalo, elk and deer. Then they returned to their villages to the east and south. By 1839, they were gone, sent by that demon Andrew Jackson to what is now Arkansas and Oklahoma; only a few who hid in the mountains to the east remained. Their fields and cabins—all of their homelands—were taken over by whites.

Like me, there are many descendants of the earliest white settlers living in these mountains who have Indian blood; at best they have a quarter, an eighth, a sixteenth; mine is a sixteenth. There are no full-bloods.

I have cousins I've never met who live in the Cherokee Nation. Every four or five years, we are visited by a small group of Cherokee who come from Oklahoma on a pilgrimage to worship in the beech grove which is sacred to them. We let them camp for a night or two by the spring. They have their ceremonies among the beeches in the morning just as the sun is rising. When they leave, there are always little red bundles of tobacco and stones shaped like animals and humans left between the roots of the beeches. My favorite stone effigy sits on the fireplace mantel in the kitchen; it's of a woman with a snake wrapped around her body, her left hand resting on the the the snake's head.

One year—I think it was around 1900—an ancient Indian came with four others. He led the singing as the sun came up and said their final prayer before they left. He told me that his father had known Levi and believed he was a prophet and that he spoke to the Great Spirit when he had his visions.

May 1942

Levi Washington Pearson was the first white man to set foot in Lost Cove. He was a strange and remarkable man who made people feel uneasy when they were around him. Even his great grandchildren thought he was scary. Lillie Jane said, "We called him 'Pappy' but we never wanted to be left alone with him. At times he'd start whispering to himself and then he'd start to singing old timey hymns or talking real loud to God and he'd cock his head sideways like he was listening to something. When he did things like that he not only sounded scary, he acted scary.

"When he made it to a hundred, he looked like a tough, dried-out piece of ironwood. He was a little bony sort of man with skin dark as an old saddle that barely covered the bones of his old grim-set face, which was the next thing to being a skull. You could hardly see it for his long beard and hair that were the color of wood ashes and hung all the way down his front and back and covered most of his face. The way he moved made you uncomfortable, like an animal stalking its prey; for the most part he'd look away when talking but then he'd glance up with those feral eyes of his that never seemed to blink as they stared out at you from way down in their sockets...he had the eyes of a sheep-killing dog. Jane Anne's husband Joe said, 'I doubt that old man's ever laughed in his natural born life...I heard him try to once, and it came out like a growl.'"

Lillie Jane said, "The only time we ever wanted to be around him was when he'd get to telling stories about the old times; you'd have to listen careful because he'd talk so low when he got to telling about the wild Indians and bears and the painters that screamed like women. Our most favorite of all was how he came to find Lost Cove. That's the one we'd have him tell over and over it was so exciting, and when he'd get to talking about the birds and animals he'd make their sounds, and I swear to goodness he sounded just like them. We'd sit there in front of him like a bunch of rocks with our eyes all stretched wide looking up at him...and you know for a moment he was a wonder to us like some kind of hero...But soon's he finished he'd begin getting scary again."

Only once did he tell of his childhood and that to his son Samuel who Levi had oddly named after his own father, a man of cruel disposition. Samuel said that as his father spoke of his early life there was no emotion in his voice or face and that when he finished he went outside to the obelisk and knelt down and prayed.

This is what he told Samuel.

His parents were a pair of drunks who lived in a one-room, dirt-floored cabin in a deep cove on the eastern side of the North Carolina mountains. The nearest neighbor was an hour's hard walk away, the nearest settlement a half-day. He was their only child.

He said his father was a monster who drank from morning to night and beat him and his mother at least once a week. When his father was away making whiskey his mother would talk out loud to God and use her Bible to teach Levi to read and write. But in the winter of 1779, when Levi was ten, Samuel struck her so hard on the side of her head she lost most of her hearing. A few days after the beating, she put her Bible in a basket under the bed and never took it out again. She began to drink. Six years later she killed herself with half a glass of lye.

Two nights after his mother's death, as his father lay sprawled on the floor in a drunken stupor, Levi poured three jugs of whiskey and a full slop jar into a large wooden bucket and set it beside his father's head. Then he took his mother's Bible from the basket and his father's rifle, shot pouch and powder horn from above the fireplace and the ax, hatchet, skinning knife, boots and two packsaddles filled with all the food in the cabin and a sack of corn, and went outside and tied the packs onto the back of the mule and walked west into the mountains.

Months passed, then years; he trapped beaver and wolves; killed deer, elk and turkeys for food; he lived with Indians for weeks at a time, giving them skins to teach him their language and skills at tracking and for sharing their women. He did not trust most whites. He avoided them except to occasionally go to camp meetings and to trading posts for gunpowder, lead, salt and fresh mules to carry his hides and furs. In the winter of 1791 he killed two Indians and a white man for stealing his furs. He left them their hair for he believed scalping to be an evil act.

Whites and most Indians thought he was Indian or a half-breed. His skin was dark as chestnut; his long black hair glistened with bear grease; he wore a broad-brimmed beaver hat and was usually dressed only in a breechcloth, deerskin leggings and moccasins with a belt around his waist that carried a hatchet and skinning knife. In his dreams he saw himself as an Indian; but for their heathenish beliefs and practices, he was one.

Lillie Jane remembered him saying, "They'uns wer a wonder ta behold, all done up in thair pretties an tha men, Lord have mercy, painted red an black an white with ever kind of animal or bein put in thair skin, you see um comin atcha through tha woods, it a put a fright on ye."

Every night he read from his mother's Bible and, as had she, he began talking to God out loud and listening for God's replies in the changing sounds of the wind and forest.

In the fall of 1798, God spoke to him as He had to Abraham, *"I the God of Hosts have led thee out of thy country and from thy kindred, and from thy father's house and will lead thee on to a land I will show thee and I will make of thee a great nation and I will bless thee and give thee a sign when thou hast come to the land, so sayeth I thy God."*

Levi told his grandchildren, "When I hyaird His voice hit drove me ta my knees an filled me with terror...but I nairy could but obey He who'd made me, an so I rose up an sought tha land He promised would be mine an my people."

Four months later, he camped for two nights with a Cherokee hunting party. On the second night they told him of a valley—many walks to the west—that was completely surrounded by mountains and filled with buffalo, elk and deer. Near the top of the mountain at the north end of the valley, the Great Spirit had built a huge bridge made of stone where the herds crossed as they came down from the sky. And they said the valley was a holy place where many good and evil spirits lived.

The next morning, he left with his pack mule before the Indians woke. He walked westward for weeks, crossing one mountain after another, exploring their crests for the stone bridge or a sign from God. His prayers seemed to be unheard; he railed aloud against the doubt and fear that the Devil had put into him. He could not eat or sleep for the dread that his sinfulness in sleeping with Indian women had caused God to turn His face away from him.

Then, on a burning hot day in August, as the sun stood straight above the mountain he had climbed that morning, he found it. Just as he finished saying to God, "If Thou hath chosen fer me ta wander in tha wilderness fer my sins fer tha rest of my days, I give Ye praise, fer it be Yer new blessin on me." He came upon a wide dusty buffalo trace that had been cut deep by tens of thousands of hoofs. He followed it for a hundred yards and there stood a stone bridge. For a moment he hesitated and looked up at the sky for a sign. Seeing none he walked out onto the bridge; at the far end, he looked down.

Far below was a long valley with open glades. It stretched southward for almost a mile then turned east, making the shape of an L. It was completely encircled by mountains. Buffalo and elk moved in the open glades.

"Hit wair so beautiful. I could nairy stop cryin an praisin tha Lord God Almighty. Thar wair tha sign, an L, tha letter fer the Lord, an fer Levi. I tell ye, I stretched my hands to heaven an cried an praised Him til I'd cried out, then I wiped my face an stood up an I nair cried agin."

Beyond the bridge the trail led down into the valley. Mixed in the dust were the droppings of many animals;

among them were moccasin prints that had been made the day before. The wall of a bluff ran partway along beside the trail. On it were painted red and white images of deer, buffalo, bear, panthers, of men and women, and of suns, moons and lightning.

The sky was cloudless. There had been no rain for weeks. The colors of leaves and grass were faded. There was no breeze. Buzzards soared upon the heat waves rising from the valley. Levi turned his head back and forth, flared his nostrils and sniffed the air over and over. He could not smell the Indians though he knew they might still be in the valley. He walked rapidly down the trail. Dust stirred around his feet like smoke.

Birds were singing around him until he reached the valley floor then they were silent; there was not a sound. He stopped, raised his rifle waist high, with his thumb on the hammer and listened. The canopy of trees blocked the sun. The air was cooler. The light was dim. There was little undergrowth. To his side, near the edge of a glade, large dark forms lay among the ferns and stones.

At the instant he saw them and smelled their musky odor, a small herd of buffalo jumped from their beds and charged toward him, snorting and blowing, just missing him as he leapt behind a tree—then they were gone— and the sounds of their crashing through the forest faded away down the valley.

For a long moment there was silence, then a wren trilled; it was answered by another, and other birds began to sing and flit and dart through the shadows and streaks of sunlight.

He followed the trail left by the buffalo for a short distance then began to methodically crisscross the valley floor, slowly working his way toward the south end, stopping occasionally to examine a spring, or a plant, or to scoop a handful of dirt from the deep loam which he smelled and touched to his tongue. In his mind, images of corn and wheat and cattle began to appear. All of the springs' waters were sweet. Tracks and scrapings and droppings of game were everywhere.

Near the end of the valley, where it turned east, he came to a thick wall of cane but did not pause; he pushed his way through until he broke out onto the bank of a dry creek bed. He jumped down onto the bed and followed it southward. Signs of flooding were everywhere. Clusters of brush, broken limbs and logs were caught in the forks of tree limbs twenty feet above him. Dead trees lay crossways the creek, some slanted downward into it; long vines hung to the ground like twisted strands of hair; patches of cane and brush grew on the upper banks. As he came near the start of the mountain, mud and shallow pools of water began to appear; around the final bend, a sheer stone cliff rose a hundred feet above him. It was covered with the same painted figures of animals and men and heavenly bodies that were on the bluff near the stone bridge. At the base of the cliff, the creek ended in a giant sinkhole partially filled with boulders, logs, limbs, vines, briars, bones and skeletons of animals. Moccasin tracks were on three sides of the sink.

"Hit wair like a place of heathen worship...hit wair not of God. Yairs later hit kilt a man, tha waters drug im down into tha sink an whirled im round gainst them big rocks an tore im all ta pieces, an then hit drained bits uv im on down into tha cave under hit; a good bit on from thaire, I found some of his bones a faire ways back in tha cave. Thairs times I'd be in tha cave an I'd git ta thinking I hyaired some one a way back in hit a callin me. Hit wair a heathen place whair evil spirits lived an hit still be so."

The bones were those of John O'Connor, my mother's husband.

A year later, Levi discovered that the sink led down into a cave that passed beneath the mountain. A mile from where he stood, the cave's huge mouth opened in the side of a cliff. Water flowed continuously from the entrance, spilling down into a creek that led eventually to where the village of Sherwood came to be.

Finally, he turned from the sink and walked back to where the valley made its turn east. As he neared it he saw through a break in the trees a small hill surrounded by an open glade. He stopped, sniffed the air and listened. He went on toward the hill, his eyes reading the ground for signs of the Indians.

Stepping from the trees into the open he immediately smelled fresh water and saw hoof-torn ground and a little ways on, a spring flowing from under a rock shelf into a clear pool. Beyond the pool, the water disappeared into a mud bed covered with hoof prints, droppings of buffalo and elk; and among them were two piles of human shat. Beside the spring were imprints of knees and hands. He knelt, cupped his left hand in the water three times and drank, then splashed water on his face and neck. All the while his head was partly raised. His eyes darted back and forth. The rifle was held ready in his right hand.

He climbed the hill. Signs of flooding ended halfway up. At the top stood a grove of large beeches. Near the middle of the grove was a grassy area and the remnants of a campfire that held a few charred logs and a scattering of deer and turkey bones. A few feet from the campfire, flakes of flint and a broken stone pipe in the shape of a bear lay in the grass. He knelt and put the palms of his hands on the logs. The largest was still warm. He picked up pieces of bone, sniffed them and touched them to the tip of his tongue. The pressed grass showed six had slept there.

He laid the pack on the ground, tied a strip of leather to the rifle stock, hung it over his shoulder, kicked his moccasins off and climbed the tallest tree as high as he could go. From there, he looked out onto the valley, studying the shape of the land from the north to the east, all the while looking for signs of the Indians. He saw none. He knew they were there watching. He closed his eyes and prayed, "Lord God, protect me from tha heathen ones as Thou didst protect Thy people in tha wilderness. Amen."

Prayer comforted him. Always. It did now. He opened his eyes and looked out on the land. He saw the forest cleared, the rich bottomland in corn and wheat and pastures with grazing cattle.

In the memory of that moment, Levi told his grandchildren, "As I looked on that beautiful land tha Spirit of tha Lord, hit come over me like a breeze, an tha sun, hit wair a pure white heat on my face, an after a bit hit felt like I wus a smotherin...I wus blinded an could hyair all kinda beasts callin like they wus a singin to tha Lord. Such a weakness come over me I nairly fell from tha tree. Then hit passed an I climbed down an fell on my face onto that soft grass an prayed.

> *Praise be tha Lord God of hosts, fer Thou hast
> brought me safely through tha wilderness to this
> land of milk an honey. An Thou hast given me a
> sign that this land be mine an hit be fer my seed
> an my generations. Hyaire me, O God, this I
> swear to Thee, I'll turn my face away from tha
> Evil One forever, an I'll obey Thee, an will build
> an altar of stone fer to glorify Thy name forever
> an ever. Amen."*

He lay there breathing in the scent of the earth until
his strength returned. Then he stood and pointed to the
ground at his feet, "Hyair, whar I be standin, I ul build
my house," and he raised his arm toward the lower,
gentle slope of the nearest mountain. "An thar'll be whar
my people ul be gathered side by side in tha earth til we
be called...An over thar whar tha Injuns stone bar be I'll
build an altar to tha Lord...An this valley, hit'll be calt
Lost Cove, fer hit an I war both once lost an now, praise
tha Lord, we both be found."

So it was the Pearsons came to possess the land given
them by God—or so they believed.

* * * * *

Within three years Levi cleared and burned half the
trees on the valley floor; a third of the open ground was
broken and two crops of corn and silage were harvested.
With a team of oxen he bought from the Indians, he
dragged logs to the top of the hill and built a double-pen
cabin. On an oak sled he brought stone from the creek
and built a chimney at each end of the cabin. In the front
yard, he raised his altar to God.

And in his bed was his first wife, sixteen-year-old Rebecca Garner whose family had settled on top of the mountain. Rebecca had seven children by Levi. A few hours after the seventh was born, she hemorrhaged and bled to death.

Four months later, Levi married Flora McGrady, another sixteen-year-old whose family lived a mile beyond the Garners. She had five children and died of consumption. This time he was quicker, within three months he married Flora's younger sister Jessie. She had five children by him and outlived him by eleven years. Not long after Levi's death Jessie married Lealer Knight, a half-Cherokee/half-white Methodist minister and moved to the Cherokee Nation. She had four more children by Lealer and died there in 1882.

I look at Lillie Jane and think, how wonderful it is that Levi Washington Pearson's blood is in her and in our children and our grandchildren; that strange wanderer whose belief in God's voice was rewarded with this valley. I wish I had known him.

In the one hundred and second year of his life, Levi died peacefully in bed with his family gathered round him singing, "The Lord My Shepherd Is." As his breathing grew shallower, Samuel began to read aloud the Psalms, one after another, all the way through to the last verse of the last Psalm, *"Let everything that hath breath praise the Lord. Praise ye the Lord."* As he ended Levi whispered, "Hold my hands fer I depart." Five minutes later he breathed his final breath.

He and Rebecca and Flora and seven of his seventeen children are buried in the Pearson Cemetery at the place he picked the first day he came into the valley. You can see it from the house. They're all buried in walnut coffins that Levi made. He also made one for Jessie but her husband refused to let her take it with them when they moved to what is now Oklahoma. It's still upstairs in the loft for Lillie Jane or me, whoever goes first.

* * * * *

Our bed and sitting room is one of the original rooms. The house has been added onto twice and now has seven rooms with a second story and loft. Clapboards cover the old logs. Twenty years ago we enclosed the dogtrot into a hall and dining room and added a porch across the front and a kitchen wing and root cellar. A cistern and smokehouse are off the back porch. The outhouse is where the hill's back slope begins. The tobacco barn and two livestock barns are on slightly raised ground a hundred yards away. They've flooded only twice, in 1910 and 1936.

Evening is starting to come. The rain has stopped. Lillie Jane is reading. I've been writing for more than an hour. The concentration tires me. Trying to remember dates and names and trying to get the words right is tiring and grows harder. I erase and rewrite a lot.

I love this time of day. Most evenings, we sit on the porch and watch the night come down into the valley. Even at seventy-eight my eyes are good enough that I can see all the way to both ends of the cove — just as Levi did on that first day. Deer and turkey are still here. They come out into the fields at dusk. The buffalo, elk and wolves have gone long ago. Most believe there are no more bear or panthers but they are wrong. For I have seen them.

June 1942

My great grandfather, James Vann, was a half-Cherokee/half-Scot pagan who brought Moravian missionaries to educate Indian children at his plantation, Diamond Hill. He had three wives, all at the same time and many children. He was a leader who signed treaties, an alcoholic and an owner of over a hundred slaves. He believed in revenge—in the washing of blood with blood. He killed many men: whites, blacks and Indians. He burned one of his slaves to death for stealing from him. In 1809, as he was raising a glass of whiskey to his lips, he was shot through the head and killed instantly. Above his grave, in northern Georgia, is a wooden slab with this inscription:

> "Here lies the body of James Vann,
> He killed many a white man.
> At last by rifle ball he fell,
> And the devil dragged his soul to hell."

I once read: "He was loved by few, respected by many and feared by all." His blood is in me. I have sometimes wondered if it was what caused me to become a killer and to take blood for blood.

After his death, seven of his slaves were sold to pay his debts; among them was my great grandmother, my grandfather and my father. My great grandmother was born free in Africa. She died a slave in America. I have always called her Africa.

These are her descendants: She had a son by James
Vann; his name was Isaac. He was born a slave and
fathered a slave whose name was Joseph; and Joseph
killed his master and fled to the mountains, into Lost
Cove. From here he was led north to Nashville by
Katherine O'Connor, a widow from Ireland with long
rust-red hair. And there, as a free man, he joined the
Union Army and was killed on December 15, 1864, at
the Battle of Nashville. His body was buried in a trench
on the battlefield with other Negro soldiers. There is no
marker.

And I, Jeremiah Vann, am a mestizo, a man of three
bloods, with skin the color of cinnamon. I am the son of
Joseph and Katherine. I was born free and I have killed
three people, two men and a woman.

When James was killed in 1809, my father and six
other slaves were sold to William Dudley. My father was
four years old. The last thing he heard as he was taken
away in the wagon was his mother pleading, "Please takes
me too Marse Dudley...I's his onlyist mama, please
Marse Dudley, takes me!" But he did not.

*   *   *   *   *

By any measurement of the times, William Dudley
was considered by those who knew him to be a good
man, a churchgoer, virtuous, polite to all, even to his
servants whom he rarely sold or had beaten. No one
spoke ill of him.

William and his devoutly religious wife Sarah were
the Master and Mistress of Chota Plantation. Both were
Episcopalians, which fit William's philosophy perfectly as

it allowed him to believe almost anything he wanted to believe. He therefore believed all manner of things that he kept to himself. His beliefs on the Trinity, if he had ever given voice to them, would have more than troubled Sarah and Reverend David Buttolph their rector.

Sarah was a good wife and good mother but she was boring. The only subjects she ever talked about were the achievements of her six children and fourteen grandchildren, and, when not them she would talk on and on about the most recent Christian commentary or tract she was reading. Like William, she was convinced it was proper to own black people as long as you weren't mean to them; otherwise, God would have said it was wrong in the Bible. She just wished that the Bible didn't refer to them as "slaves" as she much preferred to call them, "our servants." It was she who had come up with the idea of giving three of "our servants" to each of their children as a wedding gift when they married.

William never contradicted Sarah on any matter involving Biblical interpretation. While he doubted that there was a God, or that there was much in the Bible that was literally true, it satisfied him that Sarah and Reverend Buttolph were convinced that Negroes were Ham's descendants and that they were created to be hewers of wood and makers of bricks, and thereby to be the servants of white masters who, because of their race, were created to be the rulers of the South and the overseers of the land and of all colored people upon the earth.

While he attended church services regularly with Sarah, it was not easy for him to suffer through them for most of Reverend Buttolph's sermons were at best intellectual milksop. It was only within his own large library that he found minds that challenged him—the Greeks and Romans.

Every night, after Sarah had gone to bed, he went into his library, closed the door, turned up his reading lamp, mixed himself a large brandy toddy and pondered Marcus Aurelius's *Meditations* or the writings of Lucretius or Epictetus or Seneca or one of the other great Greek or Roman writers, for it was these writings that fueled the fire of his secret dream of himself as a Roman senator whose two greatest pleasures were the cultivation of his mind and the cultivation of his broad, rich fields. And if he could keep his eyes open after reading one of the ancient classics, he might memorize a Psalm as he had observed that it was a great comfort to his wife whenever he quoted something from the Bible, especially if he did so in the presence of Reverend Buttolph.

When he was finished with his nightly reading, he would turn off the reading lamp, light a candle and go upstairs to the bedroom where he would blow the flame out and climb into bed as easy as he could so as not to awaken Sarah. And there in the darkness he would lie on his back wondering, questioning and sometimes remembering his early years and how he had come to succeed in life.

* * * * *

In the spring of 1807, William bought five hundred acres of the best land in northeastern Georgia. He bought it for not much more than the cost of three good brood mares.

He left Sarah with their two little girls at their home in North Carolina and crossed over the mountains with three ox-drawn wagons, plows, saws, axes, several barrels of corn, a herd of hogs and seventeen slaves to begin clearing and planting his land. Within nine months, working side-by-side with his Negroes, he cleared and planted fifty acres of corn and fifty of cotton and built temporary cabins for his slaves and his family. Then he sent for Sarah and the girls.

Six years later, he was a wealthy man. And with his wealth he bought more land and more slaves. In four more years, he was living in a large, new, two-story house, owned three thousand acres and one hundred and sixty-five slaves. His plantation was one of the finest in Georgia. He named it Chota, after the Cherokee's sacred "mother town."

In 1862, at age sixty-eight, William Dudley was still physically imposing. He stood six feet four inches tall, weighed two hundred and fifty pounds, most of it still muscle. He was straight and broad-shouldered, with a head full of iron-gray hair and a keen, commanding face. He was old, but his strength was undiminished. He was a southern gentleman with great wealth and political power, a master who never questioned himself about his right to rule. He possessed more than he had ever dreamed of possessing, yet he was dissatisfied. His wife was a dull woman and their seven children, who took after their mother, were likewise dull. With all that he had he was lonely for someone as intelligent as he was to talk with.

July 1942

My great grandmother, Africa, was of a great age when she died in 1861 sitting in the sun, facing toward her homeland.

Mama said my father told her many stories about his days as a slave and of his memories of his grandmother Africa. He remembered the weather was stifling hot on the summer day in 1861 when the Dudleys buried her within the walls of their family cemetery and that they buried her with an absolute certainty she loved them— especially their children, who she had helped raise with all her heart and soul.

But the truth was she had despised them; she had despised her father who sold her and her brother to an Arab slave trader; she had despised the first white man who owned her, and the next one, and the next one. She had despised them all but the one she hated most was James Vann who had owned her before William Dudley. She would have killed him for torturing and burning her brother to death for stealing from him, and for having brutally raped her over and over, and though one of the rapes led to her son Isaac who she loved greatly, she would have killed him if he had not been shot to death by a half-breed.

Africa was one of the last pure Africans at Chota. All the other slaves were mongrels of races: octoroons, mestizos, creoles, griffes, zamboes, quandroons, and on and on rolled the words that had been created to explain their breeding, their strengths and weaknesses like the bloodlines of horses—words that have now mostly disappeared.

In the last years of her life, she had no duties but her own. Every day when the weather was good, she would sit on the top step of her cabin facing the sun, thin and straight with her head held high in the air. She absorbed the heat into her jet-black skin while smoking her clay pipe, dozing, watching the shapes of shadows change as they moved across the grassless yard. With her long fine fingers holding the wood that she carved, she felt the forms of animals and beings coming to life, talking to them with the old words that no one understood. She gave the carvings only to slave children—to no one else.

Joseph watched his grandmother all those years, first as a boy then as a man. Her hands as they carved were as magic bringing life forth from nothing; and gradually he began to carve, his hands feeling the shapes within the bone—for he only carved in bone and only carved things that were beautiful.

His grandmother did not sleep at night. When the night bell rang and the last lights were out in the quarters, she would lie awake singing softly in her language: songs of her people and of their great herds of long-horned cattle, of lions, leopards and elephants, of the rich, sharp smells rising from the hot earth and of the coming of the first rains. Then she would sing about Joseph, a great warrior who would one day set his people free. And night after night, her songs came through the dark to her grandson whose blood was mixed with black and red and white, and who never looked down at the ground when a white man stood before him.

* * * * *

My father, Joseph, never owned a single thing, not his sweat or his stink, not his carvings, not his little daughter—my half-sister—Dicie, not his soul nor the shadow that he cast. After he was sold to pay off his grandfather's debts, every piece of him belonged to William Dudley.

After all that could be said about Joseph, his true worth—his sale value—was listed in the Chota Property Inventory. All two hundred and sixty-five Negroes, all the cattle, horses, hogs, farming equipment, everything of value was there in William Dudley's beautiful handwriting. A house servant who could read had seen the inventory and told Joseph what was written in it about his family.

Number	Names	Age	Full or Half Hand	Value	Remarks
1	Joseph	24	Full	2050.00	Superior
168	Annie	21	Full	1375.00	Good Hand
231	Dicie	4	0	315.00	Too young
260	Isaac	61	0	5.00	Wore out

Other than Prince, a magnificent sixteen-hand bay stallion, and Samson the herd bull, Joseph was the most valuable piece of property on the plantation.

Like his grandmother, he hated all masters but she had taught him to never let it show. He was a solemn man who showed little emotion on his face no matter how excited or upset the other Negroes might be. He seldom spoke and only nodded and grunted when given an order, but he was the hardest worker at Chota. And he could repair anything: farm equipment, broken furniture, loose hinges on a door or a cracked well pump. He was never sick, never complained and never asked for favors.

His bone carvings of animals were such fine works of art that Sarah placed them in glass display cabinets throughout the house for guests to admire and envy.

He did not look or act like any other Negro at Chota; though his hair was kinky—it was reddish-brown—and his nose slightly broad, they were his only Negroid features. His cinnamon-colored skin, narrow lips, small ears, high round cheek bones and almond-shaped brown eyes were more Indian than Negroid. He was slightly shorter than an average white man with a slender body and long, sinewy muscles.

William Dudley was fascinated by Joseph's stoic manner, his artistic ability and, at times, thought he might even be intelligent. He began to have Joseph drive him once a week in the buggy to the village which was five miles away. My mother said that when my father got to telling her about the trips it seemed he remembered every detail. "That old man, he neva wants that hoss ta go mo than a walk, an he'd bring a jug of cone-likah an get ta drinkin it soons he's outta sight of tha big-house. On tha second trip tha ole man, he talk almos non-stop bout things in tha Bible that he say jus couldn't be true an bout how some peoples long ago make it all up jus so's others ud feed em an give em things, jus likes today with tha preachers always wantin money so's they can eat high on tha hog. He'd slap his thigh and say, 'Ain't dat right...ain't dat right?' Then he'd give off with his ole high cackle an I'd jus nod an grunt, 'Uh huh...uh huh.'

"Bout tha time he be gittin a little tipsy he'd git ta talkin bout dem ole Romans an Greeks an one time he say, 'Joseph, are yo a Stoic or a Cynic?' an I don say nuthin an in a bit he say, 'I knew it...I knew it...yo a Stoic, jus like dat ole slave by damn, like ole Epicte...sumpun anuthah.' An once he gots so likered up, he starts on ta tellin me all bout his sins an start callin me 'Brotha Joseph.' I's even think he want me ta forgive him for ownin us an workin us tha ways he did...but he neva say it. Thank tha Lawd he'd usually sleep mos tha ways home so's my mind could have some rest...Law mercy, I's hated dem trips...I hated em!"

* * * * *

Two days after his grandmother Africa's burial, in the late afternoon while he was clearing weeds from the flower garden in the side yard, he heard the old man's shrill voice calling him from the front porch, "Joseph...you, Joseph...come hyar!"

He laid the sickle down, rubbed the dirt from his hands, took his hat off, wiped the sweat from his face with his sleeve and walked around the side of the house. As he came to the front corner he stopped—a mule-drawn wagon stood in the drive in front of the front porch steps. In the wagon were four Negroes: one—the slave trader's driver—was a big man dressed in suit and tie; he sat sideways on the wagon seat looking back in the bed where two women sat, chained at the ankles. The youngest woman, Annie— Joseph's wife—held four-year-old Dicie their child. The women sat dead still, they had no expression; their few belongings were in bundles beside them. Dicie's eyes were stretched wide; in her tiny hands she clutched a small piece of bone carved in the shape of a lamb. She looked up at Joseph for a moment, then down at the carving.

"Joseph, get up hyar!"

As he climbed the steps, Joseph saw the white slave trader leaning against the wall behind the old man, studying Joseph carefully. He was a red-faced, smallish man; his jaw pooched out with tobacco; his beard was stained below the corners of his mouth. In his left hand he held a riding crop.

"Come over hyar so this man can take a good look at you."

The trader stepped away from the wall. He stood an arm's length in front of Joseph and slowly looked him up and down, then reached out with his riding crop, and with its curved handle, pushed down on his jaw. "Open yo mouth." The trader leaned forward staring intently, nodded, and removed the crop. He leaned closer and looked into my father's eyes, then at his hair and hands and feet; he felt of his chest and arms and looked down, "Drop yo pants."

"Go ahead, Joseph, do what he said, tha missus an tha girls are gone."

Joseph undid the rope around his waist, the pants dropped to the floor. He stood with his head high, the lids of his eyes almost closed as he looked above the wagon and his wife and daughter toward the fields and the far-off dark line of the mountains.

The trader reached down with the crop, pushing the handle under Joseph's balls, carefully moving them, watching for any sign of flinching; there was none. He walked behind him looking at his buttocks, lifting his shirt; there were no scars.

"Tell ya what, Mr. Dudley, I'll give ya fifteen hundrud cash on tha hoof, right this damn minute."

"Suh, I told you this man's price is two thousand, fo hundrud dollars."

"I'll tell ya what, Dudley." The trader reached into his pants pocket and took out a thick roll of bills. He pulled a handful of hundrud dollar bills from the roll and said, "I'll give ya seventeen hundred...hell's fire, thas two hundrud more than tha Nigger's worth...Jesus Christ, ya oughta commodate me a little aftah what I've done give ya fo them otherns. Shit, he ain't worth a damn dollah mo."

The old man studied the trader, only his eyes showed anger and that barely at all for he was a gentleman. He abhorred rudeness and foul speech, most especially, the taking of the Lord's name in vain; what he hated even more was someone thinking he was not smart enough to see that they were trying to cheat him.

With a voice, almost a whisper, William Dudley said, "Joseph, get back to work." And to the trader, "Sir, the Nigra is not for sale." He turned toward the door but stopped and turned back to face the trader, "Sir, I believe Joseph understands what I'm about to impart to you and he is but a Nigra. I would recommend these words to you, 'Everything that happens, happens as it should, and if you will observe carefully, you will find this to be so'. You would be well served, Sir, to read Marcus Aurelius for he will benefit you greatly."

"And Joseph, carve me another ring tonight, just like mine but smaller, for Mrs. Dudley, for her birthday tomorrow." Without another word, he turned and went into the house, closing the door behind him so quietly it could not be heard.

It was then that Mama said my father knew what he was going to do. He told her that as he was pulling up his pants, he was saying in his head, *It'll happen as it should, it'll happen as it should.* As he walked across the porch, he could hear the trader muttering behind him, "Well, I'll sho be shit...well, I'll sho be shit."

The next morning, the old man came out the back door and down the steps to the flower garden where Joseph was waiting. He nodded to Joseph and gave him instructions for finishing up the cleaning of the garden. Just as he finished and was holding his hand out to ask for the ring, without a word or sound Joseph suddenly raised the sickle and swung it sideways across the old man's throat. For an instant William Dudley's mouth opened, a great look of surprise came over his face then, then he slowly crumpled backward into the flowerbed and was dead.

Without emotion, Joseph stared down at the old man whose eyes and mouth remained open above the gaping red wound across his neck. He squatted beside the body, dipped his fingers into the wound and with the blood he smeared it on William Dudley's ring finger and slipped the white bone ring off and put it on the little finger of his own left hand and said, "Now's yo has nuthin of mine."

Then, still holding the sickle, Joseph fled north to the old Indian trail, which would lead him into the mountains and northward to Nashville and the Union Army. It was the second year of the war.

August 1942

Mama was born in Ireland; her brother, Timothy Lynch, told me she was their father's favorite. Her name was Katherine Ann Lynch O'Connor and I thought her to be the most beautiful woman God had created; her skin was the color of fresh milk and when the sun shone on her long red hair it was like fire upon her head and shoulders.

She was the middle of five. Timothy was crying when he talked to me about her and about Ireland, "Yer dair muther was all our favorite. We called her, 'Katie Darlin.' She was so filled with yer granda's fiery spirit, but praise be tha Lord, not his demons. Our beloved muther—God bless her dear soul—gave her tha gift fer healin."

Her father, Peter Lynch, was a man filled with great passions when the drink was too much upon him. In one breath, his furies would burst forth in mighty damnings of church and government and his voice would rise several octaves as he damned the English, which was always. And in the next breath, he might burst into tears as he proclaimed for all to hear in the pub, "Ah me daire sweet, sweet Annie she is my luv and Ireland is my blood." And those who knew him—and that was everyone in their village—knew he had failed both his wife and his country.

He never set foot in a church for he couldn't abide priests or preachers who he referred to as, "Lazy, blood-sucking leeches." Yet despite his irreverence and failures, my mother said her father was a good man. "He waire poor but generous, an used his ferrets an terriers an traps to poach from tha game parks of tha English landlords an he shared tha hares an pheasants with tha poor an needy...an fer this he waire much loved."

During the harsh winter of 1855, the gamekeepers of a nearby estate owned by an absentee English landlord caught him as he was removing a pheasant from a net. As they fought to subdue him, he killed one of them with a stone.

Three weeks later on Christmas Eve, he was taken from his cell at Donnegal Prison and hung from the scaffold that stood permanently in the main courtyard. It was snowing and Mama said, "I have always liked to imagine tha white flakes falling upon his bright red hair."

How strange and wonderful it was that as the snow continued to fall, the parish priest Father Patrick McGrath, a man with a large and good heart, walked beside Peter to the gallows then brought his body in a dogcart back to the village where he was buried in St. Mary's Cemetery. For this act of benevolence, Father McGrath was much influenced by Annie who, unlike Peter, had never given up on the church just as she had never given up on her husband. The good priest felt a great sense of obligation to her for it was she who after repeated failures of several physicians had cured him of his night terrors.

* * * * *

A year after Peter's burial Annie, with money given to her by the good priest, purchased passage for her daughters and herself and sailed to Boston where her two sons, Matthew and Timothy, had gone thirty years before to find work. As the years passed they rose from mockers to master ship carpenters, married and had large families. Sixteen months after she arrived with the girls Annie died of consumption.

Matthew took his sisters, Mary and Bessie, into his home where they lived until they were old enough to enter a nunnery as novices. They both became Franciscan Sisters and taught school for forty-two years at Red Cloud Indian School on the Pine Ridge Reservation in South Dakota. Lillie Jane and I visited them there for a week twenty years ago. It is a beautiful land. They are buried there in the Red Cloud Cemetery.

Mama was living with her brother Timothy's family when she met a new immigrant Irishman named John O'Connor at Mass. She told me that even though she didn't love him, he was a kind man and a devout Catholic with dreams of a better life. A week later they were married. Seven days later they left Boston in a coach for Nashville where they bought two mules and a wagon and set out to the south over rain-washed, rutted roads into the mountains to Lost Cove where he was to help his cousin, Nathaniel Pearson, with the farm. Six months later he drowned in a flood trying to save a mule from being swept into the Big Sink. Both were carried into the swirling waters and torn apart by the rocks.

September 1942

How can I know how frightened and lonely my mother was when her husband drowned; she was still a girl, only a girl, with no family or friends in a strange land, among people she didn't know. The mountain people talked so peculiarly she could hardly understand them; many of their ways were scary. Wild animals scared her most: wolves howling at night, panthers screaming, snakes everywhere, under rocks and logs in the fields. She had killed two in her house. Every step she took in the woods, she looked at the ground ahead; she was certain one would strike her and she would die a slow and horrible death. There were no snakes in Ireland.

She had no money to pay her way back to Boston; all of it had been spent getting to Tennessee. When John died, she had only the one-room, dirt-floor log cabin that John and Nathaniel had built, the mules, the wagon, a shotgun, her clothes and three quilts in a trunk, her mother's leather-bound Bible, two chairs and an iron skillet and pot.

Then came angels from heaven—the Pearsons.

The Pearsons, O the Pearsons! What lovely people. My Lillie Jane is a Pearson. These people loved music, dancing and singing of Stephen Foster songs; they loved their whiskey, hunting, dogs, children, freedom; they loved this valley and these mountains as much as I do.

Before the war the Pearsons had the courage to help runaway slaves. The Pearsons were greater than most of us.

Nathaniel and Nanny and their family were the only ones who remained in Lost Cove. Nathaniel's two brothers took their families to Texas in '54; Silas, the oldest, and his family were all killed by Comanches; no one ever heard what happened to Franklin; and because they had helped runaway slaves, Nathaniel and his son James were hung by John Gaunt and his gang of Confederate marauders in '64.

Mama never forgot Nanny bringing her the bad tiding that John had drowned. The shock of it was such that it seemed her soul left her and she had no mind. She just stood there saying over and over, "What? What'd ye say...I didn' hyaire ye. What?" She said she thought Nanny's face and voice weren't real, that she'd just come into a dream. Then she felt Nanny's arms around her and heard her voice right in her ear, "Honey, yore John's done drownded an so be it, now you come over hyaire with me an let's sit a spell hyaire on tha bed an let me sing to ye." And she sang one song after another, none that my mother remembered. She recalled only being slowly, slowly comforted and then she fell asleep. Though Mama stayed in her cabin, Nanny watched after her.

Nanny was a true mountain woman: tall, gaunt, bony and tougher than sin; she dipped snuff and worked like a man; her hands were big and callused; her heart was as kind as Jesus. She only had nine fingers. She'd lost one on the left hand to a mule jerking a chain as she was hooking it up to a drag. Oh God, how I loved that old woman who cared for my mother and—long years later, me.

October 1942

My grandmother's Bible lies before me, a gift to her from the good priest whose night terrors she cured. The brown leather cover is worn and cracked. Father McGrath's faded signature can still be made out on the first page, and the words, "To Annie Lynch, may God's blessings be upon you." A folded letter and two partially crumpled feathers are tucked between the last pages. From this very Bible, Father McGrath read as he walked beside my grandfather to the gallows.

I've opened it to my grandmother's favorite verses, Matthew 10:7-8, *"And as ye go, preach, saying, the kingdom of heaven is at hand. Heal the sick, cleanse the lepers, raise the dead, cast out devils: freely ye have received, freely give."* This guided her life. In turn it guided her daughters', who she raised to be Christian healers.

I think my mother may have been a greater healer than her mother. Most of her patients got better, partly due to their belief in her but mostly from her almost encyclopedic knowledge of plants and natural cures. She treated burns and bleedings, infections, broken bones, fevers, arthritis, boils, worms and tribulations of the mind. She delivered babies and comforted the dying. Mountain people walked long distances to see her; when they could not, she went to them.

Sometimes she let me sit in when people came to the house. I usually went with her when she went to their homes. I've never known anyone who could concentrate their eyes and thoughts as much as her when she was observing and questioning sick people. Even with family in the room, it was like she and the person were the only ones there. They trusted her for she had a special understanding for the feelings and sufferings of others and for their peculiarities. It showed in her eyes and voice. They felt the kindness that was always hers toward most all people. Mama's favorite Bible verse was the famous one written by Paul, *"And now abideth faith, hope, charity, these three; but the greatest of these is charity."* She must have quoted it to me a thousand times and she would add, "Jeremiah, live yair life by these words an they'll bring comfort ta ye an ta others." In this, I failed her.

* * * * *

In her second year with the Pearsons, Mama was summoned to Sherwood for a birthing. It was a hard one. The baby was so large she had to cut the mother to get it out. She stayed for two days until she was sure they both would survive.

She said she was so exhausted she could barely move as she returned home along the footpath that ran beside Crow Creek to Buggytop and then on over into the Cove. Just as she was about to sit down to rest she heard, ahead of her, the loud clackings of crows and the low voice of a woman saying, "Thankee, thankee, ma sweet babies...Maw-ree luv ye."

Around the next bend was a small woman with long red hair streaked with gray and covered with green, yellow and blue ribbons and blue jay and hawk feathers; she was dressed in tattered men's pants and coat; on her head was a floppy hat made from raccoon skins. As Mama came closer she said she could smell grease, smoke, dried herbs and the rank odor of goats. The woman was sitting on a log pitching breadcrumbs on the ground to a small flock of crows that were squawking and jumping on her and pecking around her bare feet. One crow, the sentinel, was perched on a limb above her; immediately, when it saw Mama, the crow gave forth a loud, quick warning call, flaring the others upward filling the air with their cawing. Except for one that jumped up onto her shoulder, the others flew to the highest branches of the nearest trees where their raucous callings continued for a moment; then they were gone.

I can still see my mother's eyes stretched big and hear the mixture of humor and seriousness in her voice as she told me of this strange and wonderful being. Propped against the log was a snake-like walking stick. The woman picked the stick up and pointed it at my mother and said, "Ho dee do ta ye, Katherine; me be called Maw-ree."

"Jeremiah, at first I did nay know if what I wair seein wair real or somethin I wair imaginin because I wair so tired. But she wair real, Jeremiah, an she wair tha strangest mortal bein I've evair known. You could feel her when she wair nair ye. She had these special powairs an some things she did scaire me but most wair good. Once, I saw her sew two fingairs back on a little gairl an in time tha fingairs grew back on tha hand an when I ask her how it could be, she pointed her stick to tha sky an then at tha ground an said, 'Gawd an dis Mutha erth we be stand on, dey make Maw-ree lik she be so she can mak dat bawbee back lik she spose ta be.'"

From that day on, Maw-ree—for that was her only name—became my mother's second teacher. She saw and heard things others did not see and could never understand because of their fears. She taught Mama about the world of these mountains: the lives of animals, birds, insects, trees, plants, weather and the meanings of the movements above in the heavens; and though my mother was already a healer, Maw-ree taught her new ways to make powders and ointments that would stop bleeding and fevers and pain. And she taught her the words and touches that would comfort those who were suffering and dying.

There are still people in our mountains who will tell you about this strange talking woman with red hair who some believed was a witch and could change her shape and while she did good to most people she brought pain and death to the animals of those who mistreated her. One of the old Garner women showed me a place midway down the cove where during a flood Maw-ree shrunk herself to the size of a small acorn and crossed the waters in a sky-blue eggshell.

Most people believed she had been born in a far away land and had been touched by God at birth. She lived halfway up the side of the mountain in a shack built onto the front of a shallow cave not far from the old Gudger Cemetery. Neither Nanny nor Mama knew where she had come from or who her family was.

The year before I left the cove something came up about Maw-ree and I asked Nanny if she believed the story I'd heard about Maw-ree sleeping with the Devil. She frowned and shook her head and said, "I swar an declar, Jeremiah, that's jus ignorance run rampant, hell no! Some of them stupid fools aire tha kinda people in tha old timey days that'd a burnt her at tha stake."

* * * * *

When I was eleven years old and was lost in the mountains trying to find Lost Cove, Maw-ree found me and took me to the Pearsons and to safety.

Part II

Mama and Daddy

November 1942

Four days after he killed his master, a timber rattler struck Joseph on his lower left calf, just as he stepped over a log lying across the Indian trail that ran along the mountain ridge above Sherwood. Above the bite he tied a strip of cloth torn from his shirt and with the point of the sickle he cut through the fang marks, bent forward and sucked blood from the wounds.

But the poison was already in him. Within an hour his lower leg and foot were swollen. With the help of a limb he hobbled on as the trail sloped down the mountain into a narrow gorge where a creek ran. Evening was approaching and the gorge was beginning to darken in the shadow of the mountain.

Two hours after he was bitten, his foot and leg were twice their normal size and were dark purple. He had taken his shoe off and left it behind. He began to stumble and fall; his vision blurred. The trail had steepened. He could hear roaring ahead. He stopped and tried to see what it was. He started to take a step but his legs had no feeling. They gave way and he fell forward against a dry, dead limb then to his knees and face down onto the ground.

My father would have died if Mama hadn't come that afternoon to dig ginseng in the gorge near Buggytop Cave. She was hurrying to finish; the wind was starting to gust and the first rumble of thunder came from over the mountain. As she knelt on the ground to put the last plants in the bucket she heard the sharp crack of a limb breaking above her. She looked up and saw nothing then she heard the sound of something heavy fall to the ground. She got to her feet and stepped up on the trunk of a fallen oak tree and scanned the slope. Then she saw him.

She looked to see if anyone else was there. There was no one. She jumped down and ran to the body. A powerfully built black man was lying face down in the leaves. He had no shirt. When she saw the tourniquet and swollen leg she thought, *Ah, me Lord Jasus, hyaire ye be a runnin away ta get free an ye get bit by a sairpent.*

At that moment a strong wind began to blow and the rain fell in torrents. *I've got ta get thee in tha cave.* Though she was strong, he was so heavy and lifeless she could barely pull him. She fell three times on the slippery ground before she got him to the foot of the cliff where the slope led steeply downward to the Cave. She dragged him between the boulders and trees to the bottom of the gorge to the entrance of the Buggytop's huge mouth, which rose a hundred feet above. There she rested for a bit beside the creek that flowed from the Cave's mouth, then she pulled the man inside far enough that the blowing rain could not reach him. She went back out into the storm. A short distance down the gorge she entered a stand of oaks where a patch of black snakeroot grew. With a stick she dug up seven plants and hurried back to the Cave and placed the roots on a flat rock; with a round creek stone she crushed them and put the ground herbs into and on the cuts.

When the storm had passed she went to her cabin, got a lantern, blankets, a bundle of herbs and roots and some food and returned to the Cave. She removed his filthy pants and one shoe, washed him, put fresh powder and crushed herbs on the wound and covered him with a blanket.

During the first nights she pressed her body against his to warm him. As the days passed and he regained consciousness, she found herself staring at his naked body in the lantern light as she washed him. She knew he was watching her closely as she washed his man-parts. On the fourth night she began to stroke them. She wanted him. She saw in his erection and his eyes that he wanted her.

She cleansed the poison from the man who told her his name was Joseph. When his strength returned, they made love. On the seventh day he was able to walk. With his hand on her shoulder for support she got him to her cabin at the north end of the Cove. There she dressed him in John's clothes and shoes, fed him and made love to him every night and morning. As his love for Katherine grew Joseph began to forget his vow to join the Army to free his daughter from slavery.

* * * * *

Nine months later my mother gave birth to me. As my grandfather Isaac and my father Joseph had Old Testament names, I was named Jeremiah after the prophet who tried to save his people and whose name means "the Lord exalts". Mama said I was the color of a biscuit right out of the oven and had curly black hair. "Yair Dada held ye as tho ye might break, an as he stared at yair black eyes, I could see his face turn sad an I knew he was also seein yaire half sister Dicie's eyes—an was rememberin his vow."

Two weeks after I was born Mama wrapped me in a blanket, put me in a rucksack on her back and Daddy put blankets, a hatchet and food in a haversack and they left the Cove. They walked a hundred miles in six days to reach Nashville. The second day there, two old free blacks, a husband and wife, rented them a room in a one-room shack in Black Bottom.

Black Bottom was where the Negroes and a few poor whites lived in Nashville. It was the only place that a black man and a white woman could stay together and even then the two of them never left the shack together. Though the Union Army occupied the city there were some among the northern soldiers who would have tried to lynch Joseph and drive Katherine away. Even in Black Bottom, most of the Negroes thought that a white woman living with a black man was going against nature and was committing a great sin in God's eyes, and shunned them. Few would look at Katherine when she went outside. Only the old couple treated her with kindness, but she wondered if it was only because they felt sorry for the baby, since one of their granddaughters had a child the same age.

The day after we moved into the shack my father joined the 13th Colored Regiment, Company B.

December 1942

My father died December 16, 1864, charging the Confederates on Peach Orchard Hill at the Battle of Nashville.

Lying open before me is the *Nashville Dispatch* dated December 18, two days after the battle. It is one of my most prized possessions; one of the few things I have that belonged to my mother. I still keep it, her Bible, comb, ring and satchel in my sea chest. Now and then, I take them out, hold them in my hands and think about my parents. When I read the newspaper out loud, I can feel their presence in the room, listening. There is an article on the front page that gives a stark picture of Nashville and the battlefield the day after the battle.

"Yesterday, early in the morning I rode through the city, then out to the battlefield. It was like going to Dante's *Inferno*. The hills and fields were covered with debris. Bodies and parts of bodies were still being found and buried. It stank with a moldy odor: the Confederate dead lying in their shallow graves where they had fallen; parts of men and horses were scattered in the mud and litter; the blood of the wounded, the dead and sick filled the hospitals, churches, homes and schools; the stench of unwashed bodies of thousands of enemy prisoners packed into abandoned buildings and warehouses; the burning of dead horses and the wreckage of battle; the piles of rubbish, the waste of humanity and beasts and the decay of the living and the dead. The odor of war rose from a city of 30,000, filled with 70,000 Federal soldiers and thousands of captured Rebels, hordes of refugees, freed slaves, laborers, teamsters, gamblers, drummers, prostitutes, and herds of cattle, horses and mules. Wood smoke rose from campfires in and around the city; coal smoke poured from the chimneys of factories and homes, trains and riverboats. Wagons, trains, gunboats and steamboats came and went continuously, some bringing fresh troops, ammunition and supplies, others heading North filled with the wounded and prisoners.

"It was bitter cold. At times snow and sleet mingled with rain. Fires burned night and day. Smoke drifted high above the city, spreading a dark smudge across the sky, a cloud that could be seen and smelled miles away. Where the battle had raged, trees were blown apart, trunks and limbs were strewn across the ground, stone walls crumbled. The muddy earth had been plowed by cannonballs, grapeshot and canister, and rutted by wheels and the hooves of galloping horses and the boot prints of running men who had done everything they could to kill one another. Within the city the air was filled with the sounds of crunching wagon wheels and the clopping hooves of horses and mules on the unpaved streets; the high-pitched whistles of steamboats and gunboats on the Cumberland; the chugging and clanging of trains, the ringing of church bells, the music from theaters; soldiers singing, officers shouting orders, teamsters and drovers cursing, and the hissing of campfires as the freezing rain fell steadily across the fields and hills of middle Tennessee."

The last Christmas before Mama died, she told me how she had searched for my father after the battle. We were sitting by the fire. Katey our red-coated cur lay between us, her paws pushed into the edge of the ashes. The only light was from the burning logs. I was reading about David killing the giant. Mama was darning socks.

Suddenly she put her sewing down and said, "I've been thinking on yaire father all tha day." Then she was quiet as she stared into the flames.

I closed the Bible and waited. It was her habit to gather him together clearly in her mind before she began to talk about him.

The logs settled, sparks flickered upward; Katey groaned and eased her paws forward.

"Jeremiah, yaire father looked so brave an handsome in his blue uniform...he waire a brave man, he so wanted ta free his people...fine an precious he waire." Her face was turned half away; her hands in her lap. I could see her fingers turning the bone ring on her left hand. She was smiling. "At least tha good Lord let me have ye. Now, listen ta this bout me searchin for yaire father...an do not cry."

* * * * *

After the battle, she waited and waited but he didn't return or send word he was okay. Rumors ran through Black Bottom that every Negro soldier was dead or wounded. Long before light, Mama took me to a Negro wet-nurse. Before she left she held me between her breasts and whispered a prayer, "Holy Mother uv Jasus, lead me ta Joseph today so I can feed me baby afore dark comes again." Then, she handed me to the woman, went out the door and hurried to the hospital for Negro soldiers: an abandoned, three-story brick warehouse near the river. There was a long line of women waiting to get permits to enter the hospital. The sun was up by the time she got hers. She said she almost fainted when she walked through the front door. "Sweet Jasus, Jeremiah, it smelt and looked like a slaughterhouse, like waire they cut tha throats of beasts.

"Blood was everywaire: on tha floors, tha steps, tha handrails an thaire waire hand prints on tha walls, some waire fresh an bright red an some had dried an turned black. Tha air stank uv turpentine, alcohol, blood an overflowin honey buckets. Tha fronts uv tha nurses waire covered in blood: they waire washin dried blood an filth from tha wounds an puttin clean bandages on, an carryin buckets uv drinkin water an tryin ta comfort tha ones cryin or beggin for help.

"Most uv tha men still had on thaire battle clothes an some waire layin in thaire own waste. They wair everywaire: in every room, on beds an tha floor, on tha steps, smokin, sleepin, playin cards; a few waire talkin almost in whispers; four men on tha steps waire singin quietly some ole Negro song; a few waire moanin. One man would scream three times an stop, an then scream again three times, over an over. Stretcher-bearers waire still bringin in wounded, some they took straight inta tha surgery on tha first floor. I saw two men takin a box full of arms an legs ta tha rear door waire the dead-wagon was. Most uv tha men waire quiet, though some waire moanin an one man kept callin for his mother an another just screamed an screamed. A few asked me for water but I didna stop or speak ta them. I went floor by floor bed by bed an when I asked, not one knew him. Thaire was a boy not much older than you with tha side uv his head above tha left ear partly gone. His eyes were wide open, starin at tha ceiling. They didna blink. Tha man beside him had no jaw an was makin gurglin sounds with every breath...O daire God, Jeremiah, what I saw was hell, what hell'll look like an how it'll smell...as I walked out onto tha street I looked up at tha dark sky an spoke aloud in my mother and father's tongue, 'Dean oram triaire, Thrionoid!' an then again 'Blessed Trinity, have pity!'

"It was well into night when I returned to the shack an fed you my milk...early next mornin I left again."

In the middle of the afternoon, she finally located the headquarters of my father's company. An officer told her that Private Joseph Vann was on the list of those who had not returned and that if he wasn't in the hospital it was likely he had been killed in the charge made up a big hill about four miles south of town on the Franklin Pike, and he had probably already been buried there with the others.

Franklin Pike was almost impossible to walk on, it was so deeply rutted and muddy. It was crowded with wagons and soldiers and townspeople going to and from the battlefield. She was so exhausted she could barely lift her feet for the heavy mud caked on her boots.

It was almost dark when she got to where the hill began; rain, mixed with snow, was falling. She remembered crows cawing to one another as they left for their roosts after feeding all day on the remains of the dead. The gawkers and human scavengers were departing with the crows. A ways off a mule brayed, a man shouted, "Git up!" and a wagon rattled as it headed back to town.

A soldier pointed to the hill where the 13th had made its charge. Soldiers were in the field below and on the hill still searching for wounded; gravediggers were burying the dead. Someone shouted, "Here's one alive!" An instant later, "Stretcher...stretcher!"

She walked out into a field where three Negroes were digging a grave. Two were leaning on their hoes while the third man whose face was dappled with white blotches stood knee-deep in the grave, swinging a pick with a smooth steady motion. Beside the grave lay a small barefooted body dressed in a tattered butternut jacket and pants. The face was a boy's, his mouth was slightly open as though he were grinning; his eyes were closed. A dark, jagged hole was in his forehead. His hands and feet were crossed. The men leaning on their shovels looked at her as the pick swinger continued to dig.

"Can ye tell me whaire tha men uv tha 13th be buried?" she asked.

The man in the grave stopped digging, wiped his brow with his sleeve and pointed beyond the boy's head, "Missus, you sees where I's pointin...it's over der. We's buried sum of em yestady an de res dis monin. Dey wuz layin all ova de side of de hill all de ways up to de top. We puts em in fo big ole long ditches an when we's done we's put a boad on top of em an got one of de soldiers dat could make words to write on it, "de 13ᵗʰ U. S. Culud Troops"...let me git up outta dis hole an I's lead you to it."

He climbed out of the grave and told the other two, "Ya'll have dis boy in de groun an covered up real good by tha times I gits back...now you's follow close behin me Missus." He led her a little ways up the slope to four long, fresh mounds of earth and waved his hand palm-down as though giving a whispered blessing, "Here dey be." He stood unmoving, watching her as she walked slowly past him and along each of the graves, pausing now and then, her lips moving without a sound, *Father, be with me precious Joseph.* At the far end of the third mound she bent down and pulled out a half-buried dark blue cap. She wiped the mud off and held it up and turned it, still whispering the prayer. With the cap gripped at her side, in her left hand, she walked on.

The board with the inscription was stuck in the ground above the fourth mound. She stopped at it and with the forefinger of her right hand she traced each letter. After the last 's', she turned to the man and said, "Thank ye."

Then she walked toward the pike. She heard men laughing and talking from the top of the hill. A high-pitched voice laughed, "Dat po ole Cracker won't use dat little ole pecker of his no mo."

Another asked, "Did ya'll get eva thing outta his pockets?"

A third shouted, "Ya'll quit blabberin an thow some dirt on em an les get on back, it's too damn cold an I'm hongry."

As she went on she began talking to my father inside her head, *O, me precious Joseph, tis an awful place faire me ta leave ye...me hearts breakin for ye, me precious one.* And for a brief instant she almost cried, but she didn't. She shook her head hard and walked faster and as she did, she let the cap slip from her hand.

When she got to the pike she fell in behind a wagon and held on to the back for support on the long walk back to town. In the bare bit of light that remained she saw a white soldier lying in the wagon bed. His eyes were closed. He did not moan, his eyelids did not flicker when he was jostled hard each time the wagon wheels dropped into a deep rut. The stillness on his face never changed.

At the outskirts of the city she turned away and went on to Black Bottom—and to her baby.

* * * * *

As I remember my mother's words and write them down I am thinking there is a terrible thing that enters into us when horror comes upon us. For some, it is so awful the memory of it is covered over deep within them, yet others forget nothing; every minute detail of what happened is burned into their minds forever; the words, the sounds, the smells are remembered exactly as they were. So it was with my mother's memories; so it is with me for the horrors that came to me when I was still a boy.

My father's name was Joseph Vann. He was a great warrior who fought and died to set his people free—all honor and glory to his name.

January 1943

I love Buggytop Cave. It's where I was conceived. Though it's getting harder, I still go there once a year with the help of "Son"—George Joseph Spain—and George Edward. Lillie Jane and I have made love there five times. We like to think that's where each of our five children began.

Last year may have been my last time to go to the Cave. I took a little tumble going down the steep footpath that leads from the top to its mouth. It knocked the wind out of me but thank God nothing was broken. Then I slipped and struck my knee going over the rockslide that you have to cross to get to the Great Room. Son had to carry me on his back going up the slope when we left.

Mama told me it was in the Great Room where I began. The older I get the easier I cry. As soon as I was in the room last year and Son held the lantern up and shined the light on the ceiling and walls and the stream that flows across the floor, I remembered all that Mama told me about her and Daddy there eighty years ago—and tears came into my eyes. For three weeks, they were there while Mama cured him of the snake's poison. In that room they fell in love.

As I looked where the light shown on the floor, I imagined them lying there by a fire. How strange life is, but even stranger the mind. I saw my mother and father.

The fire is almost out; the air is cool, their thin quilt of little help. They are lying on their sides, she is folded into the curve of his body; his arm is over her; her breathing is long and deep, his is shallow and quick.

He begins to twitch; suddenly he shudders violently. His jaw grips tightly. From his throat comes a high keening that grows louder and louder, echoing from the stone walls and ceiling.

His eyes flick open. She quickly rolls away from his thrashing, sits up, lights the lantern and reaches into her pocket and pulls out a cloth. She stretches forward on her hands and knees, dips the cloth into the stream, then begins to wipe his face with the cloth saying softly, 'Joseph, Joseph...wake up, yaire dreamin.'

His jerking and moaning continue. She holds the cloth over his face and squeezes it so that the water drips onto his eyes—they open wild and frightened. He grabs her wrists and pulls her toward him, his lips drawn back, his teeth grinding.

And as suddenly as it began, it stops. She places a hand on his chest and says, 'It's alright...it's alright.' His eyes focus on hers and he releases her wrists.

The lantern's light glistens on the water in his eyes; his high cheekbones and wet skin are like polished chestnut. He whispers, 'I's seed her clear: dim big black eyes, dim little-bitty hands turnin dat lamb—when she look aways din I know'd it—I's done seed it all—so's I's kilt dat ole man for all dat.' As he speaks, he turns and turns the ring on his little finger.

She looks into his eyes for a moment, then hands him the cloth and says, 'Wet it an wipe yaire face good. It's time ta go ta tha cabin.' She puts her hand in the pocket of her dress and pulls out the comb carved from white bone that he has given her and passes it several times through her long, red hair, then returns the comb to her pocket. With that, she stands up with the lantern, takes his hand and pulls him to his feet, 'Joseph, tis time ta go.'

He takes the lantern from her, holds it high and turns around, letting the light shine across the Great Room and the stream which they follow as they walk out toward the entrance of the Cave.

February 1943

More and more my old brain leaves the present and goes back into the past: a song, a bird singing, a scent, small things may take me there. When I was a young man, it seemed I could remember every detail of everything I heard or saw. But now, there are times when I cannot remember what happened yesterday, sometimes not even this morning; yet, I can still remember people's faces and voices from long ago; I can still bring them before me just as they were when they were alive—smiling and laughing, so real there are times when I call them to me and hug them and kiss them. And the strangest thing of all, I occasionally recall things I cannot possibly remember.

The other day, Lillie Jane got on to me about dwelling so much on the past. She said, "You spend way too much time thinking about what happened to you long ago, those days are dead and gone; it's because you haven't got a hobby or something else to occupy your mind...why don't you start painting or making furniture or take a course at the University or...something! My Lord, you could help me in the garden but you don't like to. It's just not healthy dwelling on all those old miseries...and that's what you seem to do...that book you're writing in all the time sure isn't helping. It'd drive me crazy. You never let your mind have a rest, not even at night. And while I'm going on so, I might as well get this said too...Are you aware you've got in the habit of repeating yourself and telling things over and over? Well, you do! So there!"

I started to snap back, *Well damn, do I do anything right!* but bit my tongue and after studying what she'd said a minute or two, I said, "Well, maybe you're right...I'll try to think something up. Tomorrow, the Garners are coming to kill hogs and I'm gonna help em...Maybe something'll come to me...I guess I'll go for a walk."

* * * * *

The next day was perfect for hog killing. The moon had come full; there had been a hard freeze for three days. I'd penned the hogs up and had them on corn for three months. The four Garner brothers were there to help me; they are Lillie Jane's cousins and one of the oldest families in these mountains. They're good people and hard workers. They make fine whiskey and don't talk a lot—few have these Godly virtues. Where it would take other men a thousand words to get the job done the Garners use a good bit less than a hundred. Zeke, the baby, is the only one who hasn't been in the service; the three oldest fought in the infantry in World War I.

After I shot the hogs, I turned the rest of it over to the boys and sat down on a log by the fire and checked the water in the cauldron. It was ready. Steam rose in the cold air. I got my pipe out, cut fillings from a twist of burley, thumbed it in the pipe bowl, lit it, then smoked and watched.

The Garners knew their business. They didn't waste a move or a minute. One at a time a hog was lifted onto the scraping table, then Zeke and Eli filled buckets of near-boiling water and poured it on the carcass. As the hair loosened from the skin, Nance and Theron took their knives and scraped the hair off. I doubt a dozen words passed between them. For the most part they didn't speak, only nodded or pointed or grunted. When they'd done with the scraping, they pushed a stake through the tendons of the hind legs and lifted the hog up to a hanging pole, high enough that its snout didn't touch the ground.

The boys stood side by side, lean as boards and strong as oak, each one held a knife; they stared at the four hogs whose flesh was white as a baby's. Nance nodded once and he may have whispered something for they all moved forward with their knives toward each of the hogs and made deep circling cuts around the necks. Theron, whose left ear had been shot off by a German machine gunner at Belleau Wood, got four buckets and placed them under each of the headless bodies to catch the long strands of bright red blood.

Theron, Eli and Zeke looked at Nance; he nodded; they all laid their knives on the table, washed their hands and hunkered down around the fire, their forearms resting on their knees, their butts three inches above the ground. Each one reached into the breast pocket of his overalls, pulled out his smokes, rolled his cigarette, lit it and drew smoke deep into his lungs, held it, then blew it out to mix with the steam rising from the cauldron.

Nance smoked his cigarette halfway down, took a final long draw, flipped it into the fire, swiveled on his heels and lifted a jug out from behind him, turned back to the fire, removed the cork with his teeth, dropped it down onto his lap and handed the jug to me with a nod for me to take the first drink. I took a long pull, passed it to Theron who took his and handed it on to Eli who had become a Pentecostal preacher after the war. He drank long and hard and handed the jug to Zeke and from him it went back to Nance who took a quick swig, wiped the spout with his sleeve, put the cork in, set the jug on the ground and stood up. The others rose. Without a word they began again.

Crows were gathering in the nearby trees; their loud crackling and squawking called a steady black stream from across the pastures and down the mountain. The trees beyond the barn lot soon filled with their glossy black beaks clacking for us to leave so they could swarm down onto the scraping table and ground to peck and scratch in the mud for the smallest bits of flesh and blood.

As I sat there smoking my pipe Mama suddenly came into my mind—I could see her as clearly as I could see the Garner boys—standing still and silent in her puff-sleeved, high-collared black dress in a small room crowded with furniture. A young Negro wet-nurse was sitting in a straight-back chair beside an empty fireplace. She was holding a baby boy in her arms; she had a white cloth tied around her head, her mouth was open as if she was singing, her nose was broad with big nostrils, her gums dark purple. One small lamp dimly lit the room; it shone on her black skin and on her large black eyes that were fixed on my mother. I could smell the woman's unwashed sourness and feel the bones in her arms. How is it that I have forgotten her name even though it was her that cared for me the first three years of my life while Mama worked as a nurse? How is it that I drank the milk from her breasts that was meant for her dead baby and feel her hands on my body as she bathed me and yet I cannot remember her name?

Lost Cove

It was in those years that Mama and I lived in one small room in the rear of Nashville Hospital where the air always smelled of open wounds, amputations, hemorrhaging and death. It seeped under the door and through the walls into our room. No matter how much she tried to wash it away the smell stayed in Mama's skin and in her hair and clothes. It never left her until we left Nashville. But years later, when she was killed, the smell of blood was on her again.

Part III

Mama and Estill Springs

March 1943

Thank God we finally left Nashville; if we had stayed we both would have died there. And thank God my father was a gifted carver for it was five of his carvings of African animals, which she sold to a northern general, that provided the money she used to buy two acres and a cabin on Elk River. It was a mile from Estill Springs, a small village near the Cumberland Plateau, which had one store, two churches, a one-teacher school, a mill and a hundred or so people, all scattered beside the railroad tracks. One large plantation named Jerusalem and a few dozen small farms surrounded the village. I was nearly four when we moved there.

It was a time when everyone, both white and colored, was suffering from the end of a war that devastated the South. Many believed God had turned His face from us. Sermons were preached on God's words to Moses regarding the children of Israel:

> *"Then my anger shall be kindled against them on that day, and I will forsake them, and I will hide my face from them, and they will be destroyed, and many evils and troubles shall befall them; so that they will say in that day, 'Are not these evils come upon us, because our God is not among us?' And I will surely hide my face in that day for all the evils which they shall hath wrought, in that they turned to other gods."*

The South was in ruins. Fields were abandoned to weeds and forests. Fences were gone, burned by armies that passed back and forth through the land. Mills, gins and barns had been burned or were in ruins. There was little seed to be had. Herds and flocks had been taken or slaughtered—those that remained were bags of bones. Some people were near starvation, their bodies skeletal. Hunger was rampant, mothers were without milk in their breasts; yet the women had found ways to survive and from this destruction their wills became stronger. The eyes of men who had fought stared far off as if they were somewhere else, as though they saw ghosts that would not leave them. They had done their best but it was not enough. They had been defeated; their faiths and hopes were shaken. Nearly three hundred thousand Confederates had died in battle and from disease.

After the war, little money was to be had; many had none. Four years of killing and destruction had made people hard. Cruelty had become easy, first with enemies, then with neighbors; families had turned against one another; old people and children were driven from their homes. Houses and barns were burned to the ground, women had been whipped, raped and sometimes killed, and sometimes they killed. There was no law. The Yankee officials who occupied us did nothing. They were overbearing and insulting. Most were despised—even by my mother who had prayed for the South to lose. The years called Reconstruction were a time of hardship that, except for battle, whites had never known. And though they were free, hardships for the Negroes continued.

Then another terror came to the South and what it brought upon us remains inside of me.

It was during this time I first saw a Ku Kluxer. It was at night. I'd gone outside near the road to piss when I heard horses coming from the direction of Estill; men were laughing, someone shouted, "Shut up!" Then the horses were right at me. I was scared to death but wanted to see. I walked closer to the road bank and there, in the moonlight were three horsemen covered in white hoods and robes. One was as big as a giant. They trotted past. No one spoke. I thought they had gone on when suddenly the giant stopped, turned back and rode up to me and looked down. He seemed to stare forever. Then he spurred his horse and galloped away.

That night a white woman, a teacher, who lived openly with a family of colored people and whose children were her students, had her head shaved and was whipped and tarred. The church that was used for her school was burnt to the ground.

Eventually, the Klan came to our house.

I was protected as much as possible from the fears an dangers of those years. When we moved to Estill my world was changed so that it was like heaven in comparison to the hell we had been living in. Elk River ran through a Garden of Eden: the clear water moved slowly between its banks; trees and cane, great blue herons, kingfishers, ducks and geese, otter, deer, raccoons, mink, dragonflies, bees, snakes, bass, bream, turkey, crows, osprey, hawks, frogs and turtles were all around us, in the air, the water, on the ground, killing one another, breeding, having babies, their sounds and the colors of the flowers, trees, sky and clouds, and the odors of the earth and of the river were always changing. At times, the river's flow seemed to not move. As a mirror glistens in the light of a flame so it glistened in the light of the sun and moon and stars, curving its way southward to

Winchester and on to Alabama where it flowed into the Tennessee, then the Mississippi and finally the ocean. The Indians called our river, "Chuwalee." Their flint arrowheads and spear points were brought to the surface by plows in the spring. Once when I was older, I uncovered one of their stone box graves at Indian Bend; when I pulled the lid off, a skeleton was lying there on its side with its knees bent up almost to the skull's jaw.

Our house was made with poplar logs. It was one of the oldest in the county. Hiram and Dorcus Smith built it in the late 1790s. A few months after they moved into it, they and their two little boys were killed; the house was ransacked and their bodies were cut open and filled with stones and sunk in the river. No one had ever heard of Indians doing this to their victims. The killers were never caught.

The story of the way those boys died and their being sunk in the river right in front of where we lived caused me to have nightmares. At night, when Mama was asleep and everything was quiet, I'd sometimes imagine their ghosts rising from the water. I would hear them outside whispering and running in the yard. Other times, I would hear them in the river splashing and laughing and calling me in their low, monotone voices, *Jerii-miii-aah, come playyy with us, come playyy with us.* I never went outside. I never answered them. It terrified me that I might see them and that they might drag me down under the water. Finally they went away. Now, though I don't believe in ghosts or spirits, when I think about the bloody killing of the Smith family, sometimes there is an uneasiness that is with me and I can even recall the sound of the children's voices.

The cabin was well built; the logs were still in good condition and closely fitted. They were exposed on the inside but Mama bought enough lumber to frame the outside in board and batten. The chinking was good. She had new cedar shakes put on the roof. In the winter, it held in the heat from the fireplace and, later on, from the stove. With the front and backdoors open a natural movement of air occurred even on the hottest day of summer. The inside smelled of dried ginseng, bloodroot, columbine, fennel, rosemary, mint, bee balm, Saint John's-wort and on and on, the scents of the many plants Mama used for making her powders and salves to treat every kind of illness and hurt. And mixed with these smells were the odors of honey and dried apples, plums and grapes, wood smoke and the river. There was a loft where I slept and a root cellar for potatoes, apples and pears. The woodshed and outhouse were in the back. Near the road, a few feet from the hundred-foot tall oak tree was a year-round spring with good water. From the oak's upper limbs I could see the rooftops of the Taggerts' house and barns that were halfway between our place and Estill. If I turned and looked south I could see the long dark line of the mountains. This was the world I lived in until I was eleven.

* * * * *

We had been there only a few months when the fairies came. It was near the end of summer. They came during the night to live under a large stone in the front yard. The stone was longer than I was tall. It sat back in the edge of the trees on the slope where the riverbank began. Mama was the one who discovered they were there. I was swinging on a rope in the back yard when she came running around the house hollering, "Jeremiah, come on...come on...hurry!" She grabbed my hand and ran back to the front yard to the stone and pulled me down on my knees beside her and said, "De ye haire them?" The base of the stone was partially sunk into the ground; its top and sides were covered with soft green moss; three clusters of ferns grew on the top.

She pointed to a hole, the size of a small boy's fist, at the base of the stone. I could hear them laughing and whistling and the whirring of their wings when I lay on the ground with my ear against the hole. They were there just as Mama had told me they were.

On clear summer nights we would sit on the porch and watch them fly from the hole—it seemed there were hundreds—into the dark: sparkles of light like tiny stars rising upward, hovering for a moment above the stone, illuminating it, then streaking away, some crossing the river into the forest where they would take honey from wild bee hives, some towards the fields at Jerusalem to milk the cows. And the next day, when I lay beside the stone, I could smell the scents of milk and honey rising from the hole into the air.

They lived in our yard for two years; we saw them only in the summer; they never bothered us, nor we them. Mama believed their presence was a blessing and that they protected us, for during those years we were always happy and never went hungry.

Then they were gone. I was seven when they left. I stayed up as long as I could for three nights straight watching for them to return. But there was not a single sparkle of light. For three days I listened at the hole but there was not one whistle, laugh or whir of wings.

On the fourth night, after I had prayed all day and still they had not come, I knew God wasn't listening to me and that the fairies were gone. I lay by the stone with my face covered by my arms and couldn't stop crying. I didn't hear Mama cross the yard and kneel down beside me. I didn't know she was there until I felt her hand on my shoulder and heard her say, "Jeremiah, stand up; they haven't gone." I got to my feet, tears and snot all over my face. She took a handkerchief out of her pocket, wiped my face, and took my hand and we walked out away from the overhanging oak branches where she stopped and pointed to the sky and said, "Look thaire!"

It seemed the sky was filled with shooting stars; two and three at a time they sped across the night sky as millions of others flickered above us in the dark.

This is how I remember those years. I was loved and I was happy. I believed in God; and nature constantly taught me. I am certain that these years caused me to later love the writings of Lucretius, Thoreau and Whitman. I am certain those years put goodness in me that never left. Even when evil came upon us, and I killed people and no longer loved God, those years—when the fairies lived with us—remained with me and somehow helped me to not be overcome completely by the evil that was around me and in me.

May 1943

Captain Robert Taggert's plantation, Jerusalem, was on the other side of our few acres. Jerusalem was spread over a thousand acres on both sides of the river, between Estill and Winchester. Even though he had been a slave owner, "The Captain" was my hero; he had been a soldier, had fought with the 1ˢᵗ Tennessee in battle after battle for what he believed in. Then, at Kennesaw Mountain, he lost his son, Bob, and his left arm.

When he came home he was still a fine looking man, especially when he was sitting high up on Lady, his son's chestnut saddle mare. I thought he looked like a knight. There was not a sign of the husk of a man he was to become.

I was in the front yard picking up dead limbs the first time I saw him ride past our house toward the bridge. It was Sunday evening and just beginning to turn dark. An hour later, I heard Katey on the porch, barking; when I went to the door to see why, I heard The Captain's horse trotting back up the road toward Jerusalem. From then on, every Sunday evening when the weather was good I would go sit on the road bank and wait for him to ride by. Mama knew what I was doing. She never spoke against it.

When he would pass me he almost always nodded or said, "Hey, boy." Once he pulled me up behind him and rode me across the bridge up to Lynch Hill where he stopped and looked at the mountains for several minutes. Then he turned the horse around and took me back to the house. He never said a word until he put me back on the ground. Then, in a voice that was sort of like the rustle of dry leaves, he said, "Give my regards to yo muthah."

That night I began to pretend he was my father. I was five.

Years later, it came to me that he was pretending I was his son Bob.

A year later, I set foot on the Taggerts' land for the first time.

It was midmorning of a breezy spring day. I was out front trying to teach Katey to walk on her hind legs when The Captain suddenly trotted up in the yard and asked, "Boy, do ya want ta get up hyah behind me an go see a place down tha rivah at Indian Bend. It's where Indians use ta camp. If ya do, go in an ask ya muthah."

I couldn't speak I was so excited.

"Well boy, do ya want ta go?"

At that moment, Mama came out on the porch, "Jeremiah, I heard Tha Captain; it's ok, so say something an thank im."

Finally I mumbled, "Yes sir."

"Well, come on ovah hyah next ta Lady, put ya foot on my boot an grab hold of tha back of tha saddle an pull yaself up."

As I did, he reached down with his right hand and grabbed the back of my pants and swung me up behind him.

Indian Bend was less than a mile from our house. Indians had camped there a hundred years before when they came into middle Tennessee to hunt buffalo and elk. It was a perfect place; the river curved around three sides of the high level strip of ground. There was little undergrowth beneath the giant maples, oaks and sycamores. The shadows from the trees' canopy cooled the air on hot sunny days. No plow had touched the ground; no cattle or horses grazed there; it had been fenced off long ago; signs were posted to keep trespassers away.

I held to The Captain's belt all the way. He was silent. When we reached the gate he got off the horse and told me to jump down. "We'll walk from here." He left the reins loose around Lady's neck. As I jumped to the ground Lady's tail swished across my face as she tried to get the blood-sucking deer flies off her rear end. The flies flew up and settled onto her stomach and legs. She stomped and shook hard but didn't move away.

The Captain opened the gate. We walked through; he closed it, leaving Lady on the outside. In a few strides we were among the trees. The air was immediately cooler. He began talking as we walked through the shadows and streaks of sunlight, "This was my boy, Bob's, favorite place. When he was way littler'n you, I'd ride him down here an I'd bring some quilts an food an we'd camp here for tha night. He loved it cause tha Indians had camped here. I showed him tha spots where they built their fire pits an made arrowheads, spearpoints an throwing stones; we'd dig around til we'd find some bits an pieces. Tha first time we came I brought a good one from tha house without im knowin it an slipped it in among the broken ones and let im find it...his eyes got big as saucers staring at it til you could see in his face that it made it all real to im. When he got bout your age we'd let him come here by hisself an camp for a night an fish an catch his own supper...that'd make im feel really grownup. He'd always bring a shovel an dig around...his collection is in a glass case in the library at the house...it's a good one."

He stopped and did not speak again until we got near to a spot on the riverbank where there was little grass or weeds. He scanned the ground, back and forth; it wasn't a minute before he bent down and picked up half of an arrowhead. He handed it to me and said, "Keep this as a remembrance an..." His voice trailed off. He turned around and began to walk back the way we had come. "Come on," he said, "it's time to get back...you an your muthah can come here whenever you want an you can dig an keep what ya find."

All the way home, neither of us spoke. When we reached the road bank in front of the house he stopped with Lady's side almost touching the bank. "Get off," he said. I slid down onto the bank so near to him I was looking straight into his eyes. He was staring at our house. "Give this to yo muthah." He handed me some money folded up. With that, he reined the mare around and rode away at a slow trot. I watched until he disappeared and the dust had settled. Then I turned and walked toward the house. When I went inside I gave Mama the money.

* * * * *

It had not been long since The Captain had owned slaves, had bought and sold them and believed that slavery was God's will to lift the Negroes out of darkness, just as he believed that when war came God would protect him and his son. He'd loved his family, his land,

Tennessee and the South and had never doubted for an instant that God would lead the Confederacy to victory because of their belief in honor and courage and freedom.

Now, all of that was gone—all of it—but most of all his precious son was gone, and he could not bear the pain that never left him. He was alive but his son was dead, and it was his fault—and God's. Even the love of his wife and the pleading of his two daughters were not enough. He turned into himself and away from everyone. As the years went by, his family gave up trying to help and left him alone in his library with his books and his bourbon.

Three months after the war was over—God had not lead them to victory—he gave his bird dogs to the Negro who had been the driver of his field hands. He quit going to church and began to eat alone, when he ate at all. He seldom left the house except to ride his son's mare. Most nights, he fell asleep in the library with his books and empty bottles scattered around him on the floor.

On Sunday evenings when there was no rain or heavy fog, he would hold back on his drinking enough that he could walk without falling, and an hour before sunset, he would pull on his riding boots and tattered grey coat and go out the back door, past the smokehouse, through the all-but-empty slave quarters and down the slope to the pasture gate where he would whistle one time, loud and clear.

In an instant Lady would appear at the gate, waiting for him to unlatch it so together they could walk to the barn, the mare so near behind him she almost touched his shoulder with her muzzle. At the barn, he would cup his hands and scoop corn into a bucket for her to eat while he brushed her chestnut coat and mane and tail until she glistened. As he worked he talked to her about his son and told her how beautiful Bob was when he was a little boy; how brave he had been when he fell off his first pony and broke his arm and didn't cry; how handsome he was when he put on his new uniform the day they left home together. And then he would tell how, on that final day, when Bob was killed he did not make the slightest sound as they fell side by side among the dead and wounded.

When he finished talking, he would put the bridle and saddle on her, mount and ride down the lane to the road where they would turn right and a mile on, cross the bridge and at an easy walk, continue for another mile to the top of Lynch Hill. There, as always, he stopped and stared at the distant mountains until the last light faded away, then he reined the mare around and rode home in the dark.

He told Mama all these things when he began to visit her regularly. I heard ever word, as I lay under the window and listened.

June 1943

In the spring of 1929, I went to visit Aunt Sally Taggert in Monteagle. She'd loved my mother and, until she was eighteen, she had been one of Robert Taggert's slaves. I went to see her to find out what she remembered about my mother and the Taggerts. She lived not far from the Monteagle Hotel with her daughter, Lucy Kada Thompson, a graduate of Fisk University.

Aunt Sally was born on Captain Robert Taggert's Jerusalem Plantation in 1847, a child of two of Captain Taggert's field hands. She died in 1933. In Franklin County she was a great curiosity; she was strange looking, like someone you might see in a freak show. When she was fully grown she was tinier than a twelve-year-old, with a sliver of a body that seemed neither female nor male. Her skin was mottled, like a painted pony's, with large blotches of black and white. She was blind. She had no eyebrows or eyelashes and only a few tufts of white kinky hair on her head. She wore little girls' high-top button shoes, was always clean and neat and had a tiny, squeaky voice.

Her daughter, Kada, met me at the door. She was a light-skinned, pretty colored woman. She led me straight into the parlour and introduced me, "Mama, here's Mr. Tom Crossley who wrote you about coming for a visit to talk about the old days. Mr. Crossley, this is my Mama...she tires easy so please don't stay too long. I'm going to leave you all alone to talk...there's some tea and cookies on the side table. Mama, ring your bell if you need me for anything...excuse me now." She nodded to me and left the room, closing the door behind her.

Aunt Sally was sitting in a little rocker with a green and blue shawl around her shoulders. She was contentedly smoking a small, smoke-blackened, clay pipe. As soon as the door closed she took the pipe from her mouth and said, "Nows, Mistah Jeremiah, I ain't goin to calls you dat name Mistah Crossley cause even tho dese ole eyes can't see you no mo, I knows who you really is, I's known it evuh since you firs set foot back in dese mountns. I's nevuh say yo name to anyone, not even my Kada so's yo is safe, but chile, while yo in dis room with jus Aunt Sally, I's goin to call yo Mistah Jeremiah cause dats whut yo deah mama would want me to...Now fo we gets to talkin bout whut you wants to know bout tell me all bout yoself an yo family."

For the next hour I told her about the Lynches and about sailing over the world, about coming home and marrying Lillie Jane and about our five children and thirteen grandchildren. Then she told me about Kada going all the way off to Nashville to Fisk where she met and married one of her teachers, Dr. Robert Thompson. They had three children before he was killed in a streetcar accident. A year later, Kada moved to Monteagle and got a job as the main cook at the hotel. As we talked of our families, drank tea and ate cookies, I began to worry she had forgotten what I'd come for her to tell me about, but finally, finally, after she had smoked two pipefuls, she smiled and leaned forward in her chair and looked straight at my face as though she could see it and said, "Nows, Mistah Jeremiah, I's gonna tell you sumpun bout dem long times ago dahk days."

"Mistah Robert an Miss Lucy wus de onlyist peoples I evuh have, cause my dady'd run off fo I wus bahn an den my mama she died in tha fire dat burn up our cabin when she try ta kill me.

"Sumpun wus bad wrong with my mama; right when I's bahn, she set de cabin on fire an pitch me in it...an I'd burn up if it hadn been fo Miss Lucy comin to da quatahs right dat moment, an hear me scream an she run inside an pull me out. She burn her own hands an arms, but she grab me up an run ta de big house an covuh me all ovuh with lard...an Lawd bless her that chile save ole Sally an raise me up mongst em. Mistah Jeremiah, I wus burn sumpun awful, but Miss Lucy she sit with me an kept me from dyin an she gots one of de wet-nurses from de quatahs ta come suckle me, an so here I is.

"Miss Lucy, she name me an teach me all I knows bout how ta cook an take care of de house. An you know what, Mistah Jeremiah, she tole me one time dat of all her peoples I's de one most special.

"Den dem dahk days dey comes down on us...an Mistah Bob go off ta de wah with Mistah Robert an get hisself kilt, an Mistah Robert lose his arm, an people all hongry an scairt all de times.

"An den one day, dem bluecoat soldiers, deys come ta our place an gets all of Mistah Robert's people togethuh in de front yahd of de big house an one of em, on a big ole hoss, he say, 'Yawl be free!' Some of de niggahs starts in ta whoopin an shoutin but some of us, we all stays quiet. I's didn't make a sound. I's jus stand der a bit an say in my head, *Thank you Lawd Jesus, thank you.* Den I's turns an walks back inside de big house an I's begin to try an find sumpun for Miss Lucy's an Mistah

Robert's suppuh. He barely evuh eat a bite, jus stay in dat room with all dem musty ole books piled up all round him an drink dat ole cone likkah, jars an jugs of it, dey evuhwhere. Dat room it done stink ta high hebben...he ain't even come out when dem soldiers get ta tellin his people deys could go. But Miss Lucy now, she did, she come outside, all mad as a wet hen, an I's hears her cussin unduh her breath...but Mistah Robert, he nevah set one foot outside. When his boy get kilt right by his side, he dun give up carin bout much of anythin but dat mare of Mistah Bob's. He didn even nod like he hear her when she tell him next day dat mos all but two or three of de good hands dey dun taken off an de mos dat wus left wus ole uns an dem dat wus so pohly yo couldn have got a hundred dolluhs fo em. But like I's say, I's stay on cause I's no place or peoples ta go to an Miss Lucy an Mistah Robert dey da only folks I gots on dis earth.

"Miss Lucy, she hardly evuh use bad talk, but one night I's hears her yellin at Mistah Robert some words I can't repeat, den she say, 'I'll nevuh sell any of de land!' Dey'd been arguin bout how dey gon to gets by...cotton wan't bringin anythin. He'd uv sold off de whole place but fo Miss Lucy. No suh, she tell im she'd do business with de niggahs first, she'd rent em land, she'd sharecrop em, she'd sweat like a niggah herself, an work side em in de fields fo she'd sell one foot of dat land. She say she'd already give up her first bohn chile an it look like she bout to give up her husband too, an she say if she have ta she'd give up her very soul fo she give up even a handful of de land...an she nevuh did.

"Lawd, Mistah Jeremiah, dat Miss Lucy, she wus some sorts of woman...Mistah Jeremiah...I's sorta wearin down fo any mo talkin."

When Aunt Sally finished, her voice was almost a whisper. We made plans for me to return in a month to talk more about 'dem dark days' and, hopefully, about my mother.

She was lighting her pipe as I walked out of the room.

As Kada let me out, I gave her an envelope with a hundred dollars in it and told her, "Kada, I want you to take this and get your mother something special." I was about to say something else but my voice broke; I pressed my lips tight, nodded several times, and stepped through the open door.

July 1943

Yesterday, I went back to talk to Aunt Sally.

When Kada opened the door, she was smiling, "Mister Crossley, my Mama has been so looking forward to seeing you again; your kindness to her last time...O my! She's so proud of what you gave her. First thing I did was to buy her a green silk petticoat, a brand new pipe and two cans of tobacco. Then, you know what, I found her a fine new rocker in one of the stores down in Winchester. My Lord, I didn't think she would ever stop shouting, 'Hallelujah!' when she put on that new petticoat and sat down in that rocker and lit that pipe. Mister Crossley, I believe you added some years on my Mama's life...and I thank you for it. Come in, come in!"

As I followed her toward the parlour she spoke loudly, "Mama, Mister Crossley is here...I'm going to the kitchen and let you all talk. Call me when you're ready for refreshments." She went on down the hall as I turned and went into the parlour.

Miss Sally's face was split with a smile. In her hands she held a curl-stemmed briarwood pipe with a single flower carved around the bowl. She was sitting in her new rocker; its back, arms and seat were padded in dark brown leather.

Before I could open my mouth, she said, "Oh, Mistah Jeremiah, I's thank you fo dat fine present you made ta ole Aunt Sally...an you sees I's done put it ta good use." With that she laid the pipe on a side table, reached down and pulled the hem of her dress up just enough for me to see a flash of the green silk petticoat. "Now, yo set yoself down an I'll gets ta talkin."

With that, she began, "Now make yosef real comfortable cause I's got lots ta tell...I'm gonna get round ta yo mama but I's got some mo ta tell bout de Taggerts...I's know'd em all cause I's growed up almos like I's one of em, cept not quite. I's live in a little bitty room off side of de kitchen cause I's pretty much cookin an cleanin all de time. I members Miss Lucy laughin ta fit de band when de new iron stove come befo de wah, I's so little I's had ta stand on a stool ta do de cookin."

She talked for a long while about her life with the Taggerts, so openly and knowingly of the people who had killed my mother and Lafe and all the others long ago; there was not a hint of anger or bitterness. It was clear she had loved them. Though she was strange looking and had suffered in many ways there was a forgiveness in her that I've seen in only one other person in my life—Mr. Tom.

By her actions you wouldn't have known she was blind. As she talked, she reached out to the table beside her. Her white-splotched hand went right to the pipe and to the can of tobacco beside it. Without hesitation she commenced to fill the pipe bowl and pack it down with her thumb. As she did I lit a match and held it over the bowl; for a moment, my hand overlapped hers as she drew the flame into the tobacco until it was fully lit. After two or three puffs she began to talk again.

"Befo de wah, Mistah Robert, he work hard, sometime he be in de field rite long side of da hands. He hardly evah use a whip on us, mostly he jus fuss when someone get ta slackin...He sho luv Mistah Bob, he luv his girls an de twin boys too but you could see Mistah

Bob was his mos special. Aftah de wah, he change, he wus a fun lovin man, but when he come home he not de same man. All his smiles don lef him when his boy died. I's thinks sumpun jus died right der with Mistah Bob when dey in dat big fight with dem blue boys dat come all de way down here ta free us." She stopped and took a long pull on her pipe and blew the smoke away from me. "Lawd, aftah he come home, it wadn long fo he done quit talkin, even ta Miss Lucy, an he quit goin to de fields; he jus stay in dat room wit dem ole books an not even readin em...I seen im jus flippin through em an he drinkin dat ole stuff out uv de bottle an it didn make no neva mind." Again she paused; she turned sideways and knocked the ashes out of the pipe into a little bowl on the table, then she put some more tobacco in. I lit a match and held it over the bowl while she drew in on the stem and after a few puffs, gave a satisfied smile and went on. "Onlyist times he's outa de house is when he goes ridin, de Lawd knows where, on dat hoss of Mistah Bob's. He jus quit eatin an shrink up inside his skin an let hisself get all nasty an smelly, when he'd been one of de cleanest white men I evah done seen.

"If it hadn been for Miss Lucy makin herself inta a man we'd all died fo sho. She get up fo de ole rooster crow an ring dat bell like it be de end of de wuhld an she'd start in ta yellin fo her own chullun an de hands ta get outta bed an dey'd all stuff some cone bread an cole meat in dey pockets an skedaddle to de fields...She done start cidin evathin: she say how much cotton, how much corn, how much wheat dey goin ta plant, an when ta plant it, an when ta get it. She make de sales an writ it all down in dem black books she keep in her room; she pick which mare ta cover an which bull ta buy; an many a day I sees dat woman out der in de fields sweatin with de hands an gittin all burn up by de sun til she might nigh black as me."

With that she gave a chuckle, reached into the pocket of her high-collar light blue cotton dress and pulled out a lace-bordered white handkerchief and wiped her lips, put it back in her pocket, all the while looking straight at me as though she could see me. She called to her daughter, "Kada, honey, you can bring us some of dat tea now."

As though she had been waiting right outside the door, Kada came straight into the room holding a tray with a pot of hot tea and a plate of oatmeal cookies. She placed the tray on the table beside the rocker, spread a napkin on her mother's lap, put a cookie on a small plate and placed it in her mother's hand. Then she handed me my napkin and another small plate with a cookie on it. She poured our tea, nodded and left.

As we ate our cookies and drank our tea, Aunt Sally asked me to tell her more about my family, especially our children and grandchildren. When we finished our tea, she wiped her lips with the white handkerchief and resumed talking about Lucy Taggert.

"Yessuh, she wus might nigh black as me where I's black. Her flesh gettin so scratched by de stickers, she look like she been whipped like a runaway; an dat chile, she keep all dat up til she start gettin hard an her face start lookin like a stone. An, Mistah Jeremiah, she get where she nevah show any hurt, but I know'd she be hurtin bout Mistah Bob an den Mistah Robert. But Miss Lucy she nevah show it, she done set her mind on holdin onta dat land an feedin her chullun an grandchullun...Mistah Jeremiah, der were times when dat chile was so bone tired she couldn't even go to sleep, an der wus sumpun else I seed she didn know I seed but I seed it, some nights when I heps carry Mistah Robert ta bed, I seed her eyes, how she be lookin at im, like she be lookin at her own baby chile dat's dyin an ain't nothin she can do bout it, no matter how much she pray ta de Lawd ta not let im die but he jus keep on dyin anyhow. I seed under all dat hardness, dat po woman she still lovin Mistah Robert. It's de Lawd's truth, Mistah Jeremiah, I done seed it all a long time ago, I seed how dat de Lawd put some good an some bad in all of us so's none of dem dat's bad dey be all bad, an since we all His chullun I's believe He gonna try to hep us out, so even da bad uns get over de river to de other side an be with Him. Evuh since I done seed dat I's done leave mos of de worrin to Him after I says my prayers at night, an den I's sleep like a baby."

Aunt Sally's pipe had long gone out, she made no effort to relight it; her eyelids were drooping; she was about to fall asleep. I stood up and leaned toward her and said, "Aunt Sally, I think we best stop now and let you get some rest. I'll write you about coming back again if that's alright."

Her eyes flickered open. I could barely hear her say,"Lawd yes, Mistah Jeremiah...I's still gots ta tell you bout my Miss Katherine...you come back...we'll talk...." Her head slumped forward and she was asleep.

August 1943

Aunt Sally was right: Lucy Taggert never stopped loving her husband. I know because I heard The Captain tell Mama about the nights his wife cried and cried and tried to love on him and how he wouldn't let her, and how she begged him to do something to come alive to her again so he could love her and their children. I heard all of this, and I heard him say that it was Mrs. Taggert who told him to go to Mama for help. All I know is that when he came to her, both Mama and The Captain were lonely.

* * * * *

After he took me to Indian Bend, more than a year passed before I saw The Captain again. It was the end of March. Mama was in the house getting seeds ready for the garden. I was on the porch whet-stoning the blades of the hoes when Katey jumped up from beside me and ran out into the yard, barking and looking up the road.

Even at a distance I could tell it was The Captain though he was much changed. He was riding Lady. As he came nearer, I could see the pinned-up left sleeve. But he was not the handsome knight I had once seen; his head and shoulders were slumped forward like an old, sick man; his clothes hung on him like a scarecrow; his long beard and hair scraggled down from under a tattered wide-brimmed straw hat. He rode slowly up to the front yard, close enough for Katey to get his scent. She quit barking and came back to me, pressing her shoulder against my leg.

The mare came up the footpath to the porch. The Captain was more like a dead man than anyone I'd ever seen who was still alive. His skin was yellowish-gray. His eyes sat back deep in their sockets. A beard, the color of ashes, partially covered his hollow cheekbones; greasy, uncut hair covered his ears; his colorless lips were thinned to a grimace. He stank. His hand's large bones and long dirty fingers barely touched the reins that lay loosely curled across the pommel of the saddle. He stared at me as though I was something he had never seen. Finally he spoke.

"Is yu muthah home?"

"Yes sir."

"Please tell her I'd like to talk to her."

"Yes sir."

I stepped inside. Mama had finished sorting the seeds; she was washing and tying up herbs and hanging them on rafter nails to dry.

"Captain Taggert's out front an says he wants to talk to you."

She looked up, "Tell him to have a seat on tha porch an I'll be thaire in a minute. Did he say what he wants?"

"No'm."

When I came out, The Captain was standing beside Lady and looking back at the road. He turned to me as I came out the door.

"Mama said to tell you to have a seat on the porch an she'll be out in a minute," I said.

Other than to nod, The Captain didn't move. He was uneasy. He kept looking over his shoulder toward the road, as though someone might be out there watching him.

It seemed forever before the front door opened and Mama stepped out onto the porch, "Good day ta ye, Captain Taggert." He took his hat off and nodded. She waited for him to say something and when he didn't she asked, "Can I help ye?"

At first he didn't say a thing, he stared down at his hat that he was turning around and around by the brim; finally he raised his head, glanced toward the road, turned back and looked at her, "Yes um...uh, scuse me...could we talk private?"

Mama pointed to the porch post, "Tie yaire horse up an come inside." She walked back in, leaving the door open. The Captain moved slowly, like a man does when he's so dead tired he can hardly move or think. He tied the reins to the post, climbed the steps, looked one last time toward the road and followed her inside, closing the door behind him.

Immediately, I ran behind the house to the little corncrib in the shed, pulled out an ear of corn, shucked some kernels in my hand and ran back and began to feed Lady. As I rubbed her forehead and neck I could see myself reflected in her eyes. And then, from behind me, I heard the first low murmur of The Captain's voice. I couldn't quite make out what he was saying. But I would in a moment.

My mother never knew I hid under the window and listened when people came to talk about their illnesses and to tell her their most secret secrets. Best of all was when they told about the really bad things they had done. Now and then, I heard things so awful I almost wished I hadn't been listening but it was all just too exciting, especially if I knew the person. As awful as some things were, nothing ever stopped me from listening. I told myself that I was getting an education about life. And I was.

I once asked Mama why people who weren't sick came just to talk to her. We were sitting on the riverbank fishing. For a bit I thought she hadn't heard me then she said, "Well, Jeremiah, thaire be people who keep all thaire bad thoughts an feelins locked up inside an then one day it begins ta poison them an, after a while, thaire never happy an they start ta turn away from everyone, even tha ones who love them. Some get ta drinkin, some stay angry all tha time an think everyone's against them, an some want ta kill themselves...You know it's sorta like when risins cum up under yaire skin an I prick em with a hot needle ta get tha poisen out. Tellin someone thaire bad thangs inside can get tha poison out so maybe they can be happy again."

When people came just to talk she had a rule that I was to stay outside and away from the house. But being curious as I was about everything, her not wanting me to hear made me want to hear all the more what was being said and every sound that was made. So, quiet as I could be, I'd crawl on my stomach along the side of the house until I was right under the window where I'd roll over on my back so I could hear the smallest whimper. And I heard some terrible things.

To this day, I remember every word that was said by one of them—it has never left my ear—a man's voice, with broken-breath words that were almost like an animal, grunting and grinding his teeth and talking all at the same time from deep in his throat as he told about burning alive a whole houseful of Negroes, "Unh, Unh, Unh...O Goddamn, I swar I didn know them Nigger children war in thar...Unh, Unh, O my dear God, I can't get they're screamin outta my head, an I can smell em. I can smell em burnin...O God...O God, what did I do?" And then, there came a long guttural groan, as of a beast dying.

And I heard a woman say she was dead, and I believed her; her voice was so empty of life she didn't sound alive. It was frightning. I thought she might be a ghost or a spirit; her voice was only a faint whisper when she said, "I died that first night. I felt nothin. I heard nothin. I didn't even smell em when they put themselves inta me. They didn't stop: black an white, black an white, over an over, again an again, an all tha faces came an went, came an went, blurrin...an a flame of fire came inta me an a darkness ...an there was somethin else, but it didnt matter, for I was dead an nothin mattered ever again, for they'd killed me...they'd killed me."

Sad things, strange, scary, cruel, funny things had been done to them and by them to others and to animals, and after awhile as I listened, I began to wonder where was God when these things happened? Why didn't He just kill all the evil people? And I began to worry that He would punish me for disobeying my mother. I knew I was betraying her. But now, as I look back on it after all these years, I realize that if I had obeyed her I wouldn't have learned while I was still young how evil people can be, and how those who have hurt others, most have been hurt themselves, and how those who've been hurt keep on living, and how most of us who do bad things really want to be better, and sometimes we are. How strange it is I learned this while I was lying on the ground under a window, disobeying my mother. I know this though: If I hadn't disobeyed her I wouldn't have heard The Captain tell about his son Bob, and later on, I wouldn't have heard what Mama and The Captain did.

So it was that it all began on that first day The Captain walked into our house and closed the door. It didn't end until three years later.

Several weeks passed before The Captain returned. The ground was damp from an early morning shower. The upturned earth in the garden smelled ready for planting,

He came at noon.

This time he spoke to me, "Boy, while I'm talking to yo muthah, watch after my horse." As before, he looked over his shoulder at the road as he tied the reins around the post. Then he walked quickly up the steps, knocked on the door and said, "Miss Katherine, I've come." And he went inside.

As soon as the door closed behind, I crawled as fast as I could and got under the window just in time to hear the chair creak as he sat down. In a low voice he began to tell about the battle at Kennesaw Mountain. The words poured from his mouth without ceasing and without life; it was only when he had no more breath to speak that I heard his voice break.

"Sherman was hell, he'd a killed us all at Kennesaw if he'd had half a chance an tha next mornin he was goin to try again. He set on us hard with his cannons an when they stopped tha air was so full of smoke an dust you could hardly breathe, you could taste tha gunpowder an for a bit you could barely see through all tha smoke. Tha sun was hangin like a drop of blood in tha sky...tha heat was terrible, it was over a hundred an there was no shade for we'd cut most of tha trees down an what was left had been blown apart. As soon as tha cannon stopped we began cleanin our muskets an gettin ready for them, we knew they were comin...it was quiet now an everyone was whisperin so they wouldn't hear us behind that big wall of dirt an logs. Strange what you remember—way-off there was a mule brayin over an over an tha strangest thing, after all that noise an explosions, there was a woodpecker hammerin away on a piece of wood just on tha other side of tha breastworks. Isn't that strange that I'd remember that?

My son was sittin by my side in tha trench, he was leanin back against tha mound with his eyes closed, his skin an beard were white with dust, his lips were so dry an cracked he looked old an worn an I wanted to touch him but I didn't, I let him sleep. Up an down the line I could hear tha clinkin of ramrods an tha clicking of hammers bein cocked an uncocked...it was still quiet but then from across tha valley came tha first sounds of their bugles so I shook Bob til he opened his eyes an sat up an he tried to tell me somethin but I couldn't hear an he reached out an touched my hand so I leaned over close to him an spoke in his ear, 'Stay by me, Bob, stay by me today.' An I stood up an looked over tha top so I could see them an there they came, seven long dark blue lines comin down the hill.

Tha smoke had cleared an I could see their barrels an bayonets glistenin an their battle flags an thousands of Yankees comin straight at us an everybody began to stand up to see, cause we weren't afraid for we knew how to kill! We were good at it...an then tough old Colonel

Yeats shouted, 'Down boys, down!' an we knelt down without a sound an listened. We could hear tha sound of their footsteps as they came closer an closer until they were so near we could hear their officers shoutin commands an their men cheered louder an louder an tha ground began to shake. Then above it all came that old Irishman's last call to us, 'Now, my precious boys, now up an give em Hell!' An all of us rose up screamin an levelin our muskets at that mass of men rushin toward us so near now we could see their faces.

There was a great roar as we all fired together an tha heat felt like an oven on my face from tha sheet of flame that burst outward from all along tha breastworks, sweepin away their first line...we fired an loaded, fired an loaded, slaughterin em in rows an heaps, killin em as fast as we could load an fire, an still they came on, stumblin an tramplin on their wounded an dead, our cannons opened on em with canister, tha air rushed an quivered, heads an arms were blown off...I saw half a body spinnin upward, they ran into our fire bent forward, veerin away then back into tha gaps firin as they came on an on right on up to us. Tha air was filled with smoke an blood an tha buzz an zippin of Minnie balls an their thuddin into flesh...explosions an concussions were shakin tha earth apart as we screamed an killed each other an I heard myself screamin, 'Kill em all kill em all!' An tha air tasted of sulfur an smelled of shit an vomit an then it happened...there was a sound beside my head an with it a swash of wetness across my face an neck an in that instant I was flung back an down hard on somethin an I saw before my eyes closed...I saw him...what had been my sweet boy...O Lord O Lord...Goddamn God to Hell to burn with me forever for what He did that day to my dear boy who I did not save."

When he finished, there was not a sound. Then I heard my mother talking, but not what she was saying. The Captain remained inside for a good while, long enough that Lady and I both became restless; when I heard her begin pawing the ground I crawled away from the window and went to her. I was stroking her neck when The Captain opened the door and came out of the house, untied the reins, mounted and without a word, rode away.

From that day on, on the same day, at the same hour every week, The Captain returned. On the third visit, they made love. I heard it all, and I watched them six times through a hole in the chinking. The last time he came, on June 27, 1874, he begged Mama to run away with him. There was a long silence. It scared me so I held my breath. Then, in a firm voice Mama said, "Nay, Robert, I'll naire go with you...I'm sorry, but I don't love you... an I think it best that you not come hyaire anymore...tis best you go home now."

He left and never returned.

* * * * *

They said Captain Taggert hanged himself in Lady's stall on June 27, 1874, because she had been Bob's favorite saddle horse, and because Bob had died on that exact same day ten years before. Aunt Sally said the rope broke after The Captain was dead. "Mistah Jeremiah, Mistah Robert done fell into de straw, but dat mare, she nevuh stomp on im; she know dat po man done suffuh enough, so she let im be."

He didn't leave a note. But I knew why he had killed himself. He'd come to Mama to be healed of his misery, but she didn't help him. In fact, what they did may have been part of why he killed himself. What she did was wrong. When she told me he had died it was like the fairies leaving us but much, much worse for by then, I was old enough to know that when you love someone there's no greater sadness than their dying.

I loved him, and The Captain's death brought the greatest sadness of my life.

September 1943

Aunt Sally seemed to have shrunk even tinier during the two months since I last saw her. I had written about coming, reminding her that this time I very much wanted to learn all she could tell me about my mother and what she knew about her death.

The first thing I noticed when I sat down in the parlour was she didn't have her new pipe; all the times before it was a part of her. She wasn't smoking and the pipe wasn't on the table beside her. I had never seen her without her pipe. It was so odd, I asked, "Aunt Sally, I don't see your pipe. Do you want me to get it for you before we get to talking?"

She sighed, "O me, Mistah Jeremiah, I's had ta put yo pipe away cause my breaths startin to leave me. I sho miss my comfort. I'd mos rather give up my toddy at night fo I gibss up my pipe, but Kada done got ta fussin so bout it, I put it down. I spect she be right...but O Lawd, I sho hope de good Lawd'll let me have my comfoht up there when I's with Im."

At that moment, Kada walked in with the always ready tray of hot tea and oatmeal cookies. She placed the tray on the coffee table, poured the tea and left the room. As the door to the kitchen closed Aunt Sally began talking.

"Mistah Jeremiah, dat chile of mine you'd think she didn have no tongue in her mouf she so quiet. De Lawd gib me a blessin when He gib me her. Three year aftah de wah—it wus jus a month fo dem culud bluecoat soldiers gon home—I's come wid chile. De daddy was bout de whitest culud man I evah seed; his name was Jack...as I's recollect it he come from Ohio an I guess dats where he went back to. I's nevah hear hide or hair from im again. He wus a sorta quiet type hisself, so's I guess dat's where Kada get her quietness.

"When my time be ready ta have dat chile, Miss Lucy done got yo mama ta me or I'd a died an my Kada die too. She couldn't get out, so Miss Katherine, she come an sees ta me an I's can hear yo mama shoutin now, "Lucy, get me a sharp knife an some clean towels! You hurry!" An Miss Lucy, she run in de kitchen an come back ta my room with a knife an give it ta Miss Katherine. I's so scared, an when I's seed dat knife, I's start ta cryin an moanin an yo mama, she jus pat on me an den she lean over an sorta stern-like, she say, 'Now, Aunt Sally, hush up an quit that carryin on an don't you move now, cause it's gonna hurt, but it's gotta be done.' Den, Mister Jeremiah, she give me a kiss on de cheek an dat calm me some, an Miss Lucy, she hol me down tight so's I can hardly move...but I's scream ta wake de dead. An de Lawd, He guide yo mama's hand an she cut my tiny openin big enough for my sweet Kada ta come on out."

Aunt Sally reached over with her little child's rough-skinned hands and took hold of mine and looked up with tears in her blind eyes. "Mistah Jeremiah, yo mama, she save de onlyist chile I's evah have. An now my Kada she take care of her ole mama til de good Lawd He reach down with His big ole hand an lift me up ta be with Him in Hebben."

Tears came to my eyes as I looked at that little old woman who had suffered almost more than anyone I've ever known; yet her heart was still filled with love and mercy. As she talked I thought, *Yes, God knows you, you are one of His own. Yes, He will lift you up, and you will be with Him soon.*

"An, Mistah Jeremiah, yo mama save me too so I's could raise my baby girl like my mama neber did do fo me. Dat's what yo precious mama done. All she do fo me she do fo lots of folks. An it not long now til Aunt Sally be up der with her so's I's can gib her a kiss from her own baby boy."

We sat there holding hands as the evening shadows lengthened outside. There was a long silent moment, then she took her handkerchief from her pocket to wipe her eyes. When she finished she handed it to me. As I dried my eyes, Kada came in and lit the coal oil lamp and went out without a word.

"Mistah Jeremiah, dis be hard to say bout peoples I's love but you say you wants ta know de truth bout yo mama's death even if it brings hurt. I's tha onlyist one left who knows what happen in dat house...De night aftah Mistah Robert die, I's hear Miss Lucy tell her bruthuh, Mistah John, yo mama wus a witch an dat Miss Katherine done conjure Mistah Robert an stole im away, make im not see her, not hear her heart. She say yo mama's doins with Mistah Robert same as yo mama hangin im herself. She tell Mistah John dat Miss Katherine done kill Mistah Robert. An Mistah John he say he see ta it. She say de Bible say a witch not spose ta live. He say he see ta it. She say, 'God bless you, brothuh.' Dat's what dey say. An when I's hear it, I knows Miss Lucy mean ta bring harm on yo mama cause Mistah John he wus de head Ku Kluxuh. An der yo mama not knowin dat ole man wus goin ta do her harm, dat she wus all by herself but fo you, an you be only a boy. Dem wus awful times, de ole Debil wus roamin all round dis earth an he done took a hold on Miss Lucy."

She pulled the right sleeve of her dress up an held her arm out to the light. "Mistah Jeremiah, look at my po ole flesh. You see dat? I wus on fire when Miss Lucy run inta dat cabin an it burnin all round her an she wrap her shawl round me an she smothuh tha flames an carry me out. She save me, den she raise me an teach me things so's I's not a burden but I's worth sumpun. All dem years aftah de wah without any help from Mistah Robert done turn Miss Lucy hahd.

"Dat night when Mistah John keep sayin he'd see ta it, I know what he mean ta do...he mean de Kluxuhs dey gwine ta go ta yo mama an dey gonna hurt her. So's I sneak out an run ta yah'lls house an tells yo mama dey a comin an when I do, her eyes get ta lookin off sumwheres else. She ain't scared lookin a bit...den she say, 'God bless you, Sally—now yo get on back so's dey don see you,' an she push me out de do an close it.

"I's runs back an jus barely as I's get in de shadows by de side of de big house I's hears de hawses comin from de barn an dey pass de house an go on down de lane toward yo house...an O my Lawd, Mistah Jeremiah, I's hear Miss Lucy's voice tellin Mistah John sumpun as dey pass by.

"I's so scared I's could barely gets air in me. I's gets up on de poch an looks cross de fields toward yo house an sees little bits uv light, but I's don hear a sound, cept maybe onst I's hears Mistah John but I's cain't make it out an aftah a long while waitin, I goes on ta my bed an covers my head an I prays till I goes ta sleep."

She paused, shook her head and clenched her handkerchief between both hands. "What dey did ta yo mama still weigh heavy on my heart." She looked away, "What dey did wus a bad thing...a bad, bad thing." In the lamplight, I could see tears streaking her cheeks. "I jus don't understand, cause dey's all so good ta me: Miss Lucy, Mistah Robert, de boys...she gib me life, jus like yo mama gib me life, so's I loves em both an I loves em still.

"Mistah Jeremiah, you a smart man, can you tell dis ole culud woman why my God who lubs His chullun, let dem peoples do dem awful things to yo mama?"

And then, as a mother does with her child, she reached out with her left hand and felt my cheeks and with the handkerchief in her right she wiped my tears away. "Chile...de Lawd Jesus be our Savior an I's trust Him to wipe all de tears away dat dis ole world bring on us...Mistah Jeremiah, yo sweet mama be inside us both, an ole Sally goin ta see her again soon."

Aunt Sally's face and body were tired and quiet. It was dark outside. In the light of the coal oil lamp I could see her upper body rising and falling as she breathed. I told her it was time for me to go so she could get some rest. She nodded but did not speak. I rose as quietly as I could, leaned over and kissed her on her cheek and walked toward the door to the hall. I stopped there, turned and said, "Aunt Sally, Mama stayed behind so I could get away."

Aunt Sally died in 1933. She is buried in the small colored section at the back of the Monteagle Cemetery.

October 1943

Even though I was a boy when it all happened, and even though I loved my mother dearly, there was a long time in my life when I believed what she had done with Captain Taggert was wrong, and that she was partly to blame for his death—but as I grew older and committed my own sins I began to think, who am I to stand in judgment of my mother who had loved me and cared for me without anyone's help, and who am I to judge anyone, even the Taggerts, for I have done terrible things in my life: I've been lascivious and a drunkard, and I've cursed God, and I've killed three people—so who am I to judge another?

* * * * *

Terror. Total, unbelievable terror, if prolonged, never dies within the mind. The horrors created are always there. Years later. Long years later. The sounds, the smells, the touch, everything seen and felt can return in an instant. Here. Now. So it was and is with me about the night the Taggerts came to our cabin carrying torches.

I was asleep when Mama shook me awake. I started to speak and she clamped her hand over my mouth and whispered, *"Be quiet, don't say naire a thing."* She pulled me out of bed, grabbed my shirt and pants, gave them to me and pushed me down the ladder from the loft to the back door.

Katey had left her six just-born puppies in the shed; she was running back and forth on the front porch, barking and growling. Horses were galloping around the house, snorting and blowing. Riders, with hoods on, were yelling and cursing. A woman screamed, "Come out, you whorin murderah...an bring your niggah bastad boy with ya!" Their torches flickered on the window. Mama cracked the back door open, looked outside and gave me a quick kiss on the cheek; there was fear in her voice as she whispered, *"Jeremiah, run an hide in tha cane an don't come out or make a sound til I call you...now run!"*

I took off across the yard as fast as I could go and hid in the dark behind the trunk of a tree just in time for at that very moment, a horse came around the side of the house. The rider was a small man. He was holding a torch. His head was covered with a hood. When his horse wheeled to face the house and his back was to me, I came from behind the tree and ran through the woods to the riverbank, leaped down its side into the cane, curled up in a ball on the ground and pressed my hands to my mouth to cover my sobbing.

I hadn't laid there more than a minute or so before I heard the slow hoof falls of a horse coming along the top of the bank. It stopped right above me. The light from a torch flickered through the cane. For a moment there was dead silence, then the loud, deep voice of John Gaunt, the High Sheriff of Franklin County, called out, "Je'miah, whah ah ya? Yo mama wants ya ta come on back in now."

I held my breath and squeezed my eyes shut and didn't move. It was quiet again for a long while. Then he shouted, this time with anger in his voice, "Boy, yo come hyah ta me right now!"

And it was quiet again but only for a moment, then the horse began walking away. I didn't move; I barely breathed. In a while the horse and the flickering light returned. "Damnit boy, yo come hyah now! Yo mama needs ya!" Then he whispered, "*Goddamit to hell ya little niggah, I'll get ya latah an when I do....*"

From the direction of the house the woman hollered, "Come on, John, let's get it over with an go!" This time the voice of John Gaunt's sister, Lucy Taggert, was clear and distinct.

The sound of the horse's hooves grew fainter and fainter as it headed back to the house. Finally, it was quiet but for the deep *jug-o-rum, jug-o-rum* of bullfrogs and the splashing of fish.

I slept. And the dream came that has never left me.

The Great Blue Heron does not move. It stands absolutely still, peering downward into the water, its spear-like beak set to strike.

Across the river, on the opposite bank hidden in the cane, a boy watches. He is as tall as the heron and as beautiful.

The morning sun burns away the river's mist. It warms the boy like a blanket.

The heron's black eye stripe sweeps backward across the white head.

The boy slumps sideways. His eyes droop and close.

'Wake! Wake up! They're outside. Hurry! Run to the cane and hide. Keep quiet. I'll find you. Run!'

He runs in darkness through the slashing cane to the edge of the river.

In the morning light he sees himself asleep and he sees the heron's beak in one quick smooth motion spear downward into the water then out and a glittering fish twists high in the air and is caught in the beak and swallowed. Then the heron begins its stalk again, moving steadily through the shallow water with its long neck stretched outward while its eyes search below the murky surface.

It stops, turns its head and looks straight across the river at the boy. Through the green cane its yellow eyes see the boy's black eyes staring back. For a long moment they stare at one another.

Then the heron gives a deep, harsh cry and leans forward. It takes a few steps, spreads its broad wings and strokes the air powerfully and flies slowly up the river with its long legs stretched out behind.

A kingfisher's loud *rickety, crick, crick, crick* woke me. For a moment I thought I was still dreaming, then I felt the mosquito bites, the sting from the cane's cuts and the burning of the sun, and all of it came back to me: the galloping horses, the shouts, the burning torches and Mama telling me to run and hide in the cane.

Mama was not there.

The sun stood straight up in the sky.

I was blinded by the light.

The air was still and burning hot and muggy.

Crows called in the distance.

A fish splashed.

Mama had not come.

I sat up, alert and frightened. Other than the crows and fish and the buzzing of insects, it was quiet. I heard no horses or talking. *Where was Mama?* I was so stiff and weak I had to hold to a stalk of cane to stand up. When my strength returned I climbed the bank. At the top, I turned right and started back through the woods toward the house.

The dry grass crunched under my feet.

Large hoof prints in the dust led toward the house.

No birds were singing.

The closer I got to the house the more frightened I became. I kept repeating over and over, *Our Father which art in Heaven, Our Father which art in Heaven...*I took a deep breath and ran through the woods until I reached the edge of the backyard where the shed stood. I pressed my body up against the warm boards of the shed's back wall where I could see between the cracks.

Sunlight came through the open door onto the straw bed in a corner where Katey's new puppies stayed. They weren't there. *Katey...Katey,* I whispered. I breathed deeply then whistled softly three times. Nothing. Then I whistled louder. Nothing. The puppies did not whimper. Katey did not come or bark.

From the corner of the shed I could see the back door of the house. I whistled as loud as I could. The back door did not open. Mama did not come out or call me. *Where is she? She said she'd come. Where is she?* I listened for a long while but heard only the humming of insects.

Suddenly, one bird sang: Mama's pet mockingbird that lived in the sourwood tree beside the house. Its sound was loud and strident. It sang and sang and sang, then stopped.

The Lord is my Shepherd...the Lord is my Shepherd.

I stepped from behind the shed into the sun and walked cautiously across the dirt-packed yard to the back steps, up them, opened the door and entered the dimly lit room. Coming out of the bright sunlight I could not see clearly. I rubbed my eyes, opened them and saw the smashed furniture and clothing and quilts torn in shreds, broken glass and pottery littering the floor, and crushed baskets, dried herbs and roots thrown in the fireplace, pictures slashed, books torn apart, the iron stove on its side, ashes and flour covering everything: the window was broken; the front door hung loosely on its hinges. I worked my way through the destruction and climbed the ladder to the loft. As below, it was wrecked. Aimlessly, I lifted pieces of furniture and pushed rubble around with my feet as though I might find something, I did not know what; maybe something that would help find her. *Where is she? Where is she? Where could she be?*

All I wanted was my mother. I knew she was hiding somewhere, but where? *Maybe she's hurt and waiting for me to find her.*

In a daze, I stumbled over the stove, fell forward and cut my hands but felt no pain. I got up, looked around a last time, opened the front door and walked out on the porch.

I took one step and my feet slid from under me and I fell face down into slime that was thick as molasses. A loud drone and buzzing rose around me as hundreds of large green flies swarmed upward from something lying right beside me. The flies lit on my face and hands.

The fall knocked the air out of me; for a moment I couldn't comprehend what the thing was lying next to my face. And then, the horror of what I saw took my breath away: Katey's empty eyes staring into mine as bloated flies crawled in and out of her open mouth; the fetid stench of her entrails spilling from the wide gash in her stomach filled the air.

Even now, as I write this, I see the fixed stare in her gentle eyes; I hear the buzzing of the flies; I smell the stench spreading into my lungs and skin and clothing; and, again, the terror and loneliness that I felt that night and day returns—terror worse than any other I would ever feel, even that which was to come three years later.

My hands were pressed into the blood. It squeezed up between my fingers.

My face lifted.

I pushed myself up as fast as I could without slipping back down into the death that was on me. I got to my knees, braced one hand against the wall, stood and taking two long strides, jumped down onto the yard and began turning in circles screaming, "Mama! Mama! Mama!" until I could scream no more.

Did I pass out? I think I did for a moment.

Fear, heat and dehydration were taking over me. Holding to the side of the house I slowly made my way to the well in the backyard. I was so weak I could barely draw a bucket of water to the rim. Much of it spilled as I set it on the ground. I got down on my hands and knees, stuck my head into the bucket and drank and drank until I could drink no more. When I finished I felt nothing; I had no sensation of movement as I went a little ways back into the shade of the trees behind the shed and dropped to the ground. At that instant I heard men's voices and horses coming around the house into the backyard.

"Goddamnit...shut up, Sam, go in thah an look!" The voice of John Gaunt.

"Yassuh, ole Massa Uncle John," answered Sam, one of Lucy Taggert's twin boys.

"An quit callin me 'ole Massa', Goddamnit!"

"Come on Uncle John, I's jus funnin ya."

Leather squeaked. Horses snorted and stomped. There was a loud crash inside the cabin, "Damn, it stinks in hyar!"

"It's hotter'n hell. I gotta have a drink," said Hubert, Sam's twin.

Again, there was a squeaking of leather.

The well's pulley rattled as the bucket lowered and squealed as it was raised, filled with water.

"Hyar ye go Uncle, getcha a drink."

"Thank ya. Damn thas good!"

A horse snorted and pawed the ground.

"Goddamn these flies!"

"Sam, ya wanna drink of water?"

"Yeh... Thank ya. Damn, thas awful good!"

"Sam, better check that shed while you're down."

The horses' snortings and stompings were constant.

"Sistah's madder'n hell bout ya'll bringin those pups home."

"Ah hell, tha kids love em...ain't nothin in tha shed."

Again, there was the squeak of leather. A horse nickered.

"Uncle John, les get outta hyar. I got stink all ovah me."

"Damn these flies are eatin me alive!"

"You snivelin shits!" John Gaunt exploded, "Can't you get it through yo heads that that niggah bastahd boy knows us, so's we bettah find im. That bitch-Devil mama of his fornicated yo daddy an same as hung im herself, but that won't make no mind to no Jedge if tha boy talks...an I promised yo mama that that Devil's spawn's time's come jes like his mama's came...I guess he's gone; but he couldn't have got far, ya'll see bout gettin them trackin dogs from that niggah coon huntah tomorrow...they'll find im."

The horses moved off toward the front yard. There was laughter.

I lay there a long time, scareder than I had ever been for Mama. I knew about her and The Captain and about him hanging hisself but I couldn't see why they wanted to kill us for it cause Mama didn't hang him; he'd hung hisself.

We had to get away. If we didn't, they'd come back and kill us both.

The sun had passed its midway point; it was midafternoon, the hottest part of the day. There was no movement in the air. The humidity was heavy. Even the mockingbird was silent. The shrill stridulations of katydids were the last sounds as I fell asleep.

When I awoke the sun was low in the sky. The first dusk of evening would soon dim the light. One quick breeze touched my face. Immediately I was listening for sounds of the horses returning. There were none. The katydids were silent. A quail whistled once and was silent from the field beyond the wood. I forced myself to stand and went to the well, drew water and drank, pouring the rest over my body. Though my head was clearer I didn't know what to do: stay at the house or start searching up and down the river? I went around the house to the front yard and squatted down between the roots of the massive white oak next to the road. From there I could see up and down the road and hear the hoof beats if they returned.

The oak tree's broad shadow spread across the road and yard. Here and there, the shadow was broken by dapples of light. I sat with my head slumped, staring at the ground, my arms resting on my bent knees. *What should I do? Where should I go?* The images and sounds of the night and day went over and over in my mind.

I could feel the beginning of panic in me when, beneath my legs, I noticed a line of small black ants scurrying back and forth on the ground. They were coming from a hole in a pyramid of dirt a yard away from the tree's roots. The line wound its way between clumps of dry grass to a cluster of dark spots a few inches in front of my feet; the spots were barely seeable in the broken shadows. Now and then, one ant would pause with its antenna twitching, telling something to the others. They all knew where they were going and what they were doing. My eyes fixed on them.

Was it only a few minutes that passed...a half hour? Longer? A second breeze came. This one rustled the oak's leaves. There was an alteration of light and shadow, an almost imperceptible shifting, a slight turning of darkness over the ants. It happened but for an instant, then it was gone and the shadow was still. The ants continued their steady streaming back and forth. I watched them.

There was a third breeze, this one stronger. I saw the shadow shift again; this time it moved all the way across my feet and hands.

I looked up into the tree.

There, not far above me, among the limbs and leaves, a shape was twisting. Flickers of light shone round its edges. I rubbed my eyes and looked again.

The last of the day's light glittered on her long red hair.

The sun was starting to set. To the west the sky was streaked red and gold. I cut the rope from around her neck and brought my mother down to the ground as gently as I could. I dragged her body across the yard and into the cabin and laid her on a torn quilt.

She was covered with bruises and cuts and dried blood. Her neck and wrists were purple and black from the ropes. Her body was swollen from the heat. Her dress was torn and filthy with dirt and blood.

I filled the well bucket with water and took some pieces of cloth and cleaned her the best I could and put a clean dress on her. On the floor, I found the box where she kept the old newspaper about the Battle of Nashville and the white bone comb that my father had carved for her—I combed her hair. When I was finished I sat beside her and held her hand and thought of her as she had been and I listened to her telling about the snows in Ireland, about Buggytop, about the fairies and about her search for my father. I did not cry or pray; there were no tears or prayers left in me. I sat til darkness came. Then I rose, found a knife, cut a long lock of her hair and folded it into her Bible. I slipped the bone ring off her finger and put it in the box with the comb. Then I put the box, her Bible, some bread, bacon and a gourd of water into a haversack.

Just outside the door, in the trees next to the river, two screech owls called and I heard her voice as clear as the owls, *Jeremiah, they aire callin ta those who've gone on. They aire tellin them that you aire still hyaire. They aire tellin them....*

I sat back down next to Mama, took her hands in mine and thought of all the stories she had told me of my father and of her life; and I thought of all she had taught me and of her hard work, our laughter, our teasing; it all came to me: image after image, sound after sound. I closed my eyes and heard her say once more, *O Jeremiah, yaire so like yaire Dada...me precious, precious boy, how dairly I love thee.* I could see her freckled smile that made two deep dimples beside her mouth; and I could hear her laughter and her Irish accent calling me from her wild flower garden on the bank of the river, *Come see tha spider lilies, tis beautiful they aire.* And as I came to her she brought her hands filled with white slender blossoms from behind her back and thrust them at my face laughing, *Aha, me boy, now ye've white spiders all over yaire face.*

Yes, I hear her voice now as clearly as I heard it then. Yes, I'll hear her calling me when the spider lilies bloom in the spring and the sky is all blue and beautiful. Yes, I hear her whispering in my ear, *I love ye, Jeremiah.* And yes! I answer her, and will answer her always, "I love you, Mama."

I bent over and kissed her on the tip of her nose. She'd loved that; it tickled and caused her nose to twitch and made us laugh.

I stood up and shook the ashes off a torn sheet and covered her completely. In the corner of the room I found a jug that was filled with coal oil and I pulled the stopper out and began to quickly shake the coal oil over the sheet and the broken furniture. Then I backed away to the front door. I struck a match and held the flame to a page I had torn from the back of the Bible. When it was almost engulfed in fire, I pitched it into the room.

In minutes, the inside of the cabin filled with flames. I turned away, hung the haversack over my shoulder and walked out to the road and turned toward the bridge. When I reached it I looked back. The flames were high above the cabin; their light lit the river and the trees along the bank. Near the top of the tallest tree I could see a heron sitting on its nest. For an instant, I thought I saw the flames reflecting in its eye. Then I began walking toward the mountains and never looked back.

Part IV

Lafe

November 1943

As I crossed the river and headed south toward the mountains the stars were my only light. Keeping away from houses and barns, I stayed in the woods wherever I could. Fear shortened my breath. I was exhausted but kept walking to get as far away as I could before morning.

When the first light of dawn came I was at the end of a long pasture that ended where the forest and the foot of the mountains began. Boulders were scattered around in the short-cropped grass. A short distance away, a flock of ewes grazed; their lambs ran and leaped around them. A whiff of decaying flesh rose from a gully that extended from the trees into the field. The gully was overgrown with brush and blackberry briars and strewn with the bleached bones of sheep and two rotting carcasses. A split rail fence snaked around the field crossing the gully at the tree line. I climbed the fence to get into the protection of the trees. There I stopped, sat down by the gully, drank from the gourd and ate half of a raw potato. Looking back toward the field, I saw the sheep milling together, the lambs pushing against their mothers. They were all turned facing a large gray fox crossing the field. The fox never looked toward them but disappeared into its den under a pile of fieldstones at the edge of the woods.

There was not a breath of air; even the shade was hot and muggy. Flies were everywhere. The sheep had returned to grazing. The only sound was the bleating of the lambs. Dozens of buzzards circled above, now and then dipping down low over the field. With their long wings spread wide, three of them glided down and lit on the grassless rim at the far end of the gully. They watched me as I slid down the bank and crawled under the brush and briars and began to pick and eat the berries.

I had been there only moments when I heard a horse snort and the voice of John Gaunt out in the field, a short way below the gully.

"Goddamn that niggah, sho as hell he was lyin to ya bout losin them dogs. You should uv put tha whip to his black ass."

"Well damn, Uncle, I tried. I slapped im a couple of times, but all he'd say was, they'us lost. Shit, I'm sorry," answered Sam.

"Well sorry ain't gonna get im...an we sho as hell bettah get im cause he could get yore sorry asses hung an mine too!"

"Aw, don't worry, Uncle John, we'll ketch im," said Hubert.

"Damnit, it stinks hyah," said Sam.

"Ah hell, les backtrack an see if we can pick up where he turned off."

The ewes and lambs had grown silent when the killers rode up but as the sound of the horses' hooves faded their, "nahaaaaa...nahaaaaa...nahaaaaaa" to one another returned. I fell asleep thinking, *I'll kill John Gaunt, I'll kill all of em.*

When I awoke it was dark. Owls and whippoorwills were calling. I crawled out of the gully, my clothes torn, my hands and arms scratched; I smelled of death. I drank the last of the water. Barely able to see with the light of the stars and moon, I started up the mountain on a deer trail that twisted steeply upward between boulders and fallen trees, around laurel hells and sheer walls of stone.

Tripping and falling, cutting my hands, bruising my knees and arms, tearing my clothes even more, I climbed upward and reached the top in the dim first light of morning.

I crossed a rutted wagon road that ran along the middle of the crest. There was an odor of wood smoke. From nearby came the lowing of a milk cow and the barking of a dog. It was easier walking as the ground was level and the trees were thinned. I broke into a trot and quickly got to the far side of the crest where the forest covered me. The slope there was steep and it dropped into a deep gorge filled with boulders and fallen trees. As I started down, the sound of falling water masked all other sounds. There was no sign another human had ever been there: no footpath, no blazes, no ax-felled trees. The ground was wet and slippery and difficult to get through because of the labyrinth of stones and trees.

When I neared the bottom I was so exhausted I couldn't go on. My feet were bleeding and covered with blisters, the flesh on my hands was so raw I could barely grip the trees and limbs for support and the sores on my legs and lower body were swollen and filled with puss. I was lost and so weak I knew I was going to fall if I continued; I eased down on my knees and crawled into the opening of a giant hollow chestnut, curled up and again was instantly asleep.

I smelled her before I saw her—odors, odors, odors— wood smoke, goats, mint, fresh-turned earth, grease and the sourness of an unwashed body. Hunkered down in the opening of the log, almost within arms reach, I saw something that was like an old woman, a strange thing dressed in tattered men's clothing: filthy gold-striped pants, a dark blue cavalry jacket, barefooted. Thin, splotched hands rested on high-bent knees, her head thrust forward. Long faded red hair, streaked gray, with crow and hawk feathers tied into a single pigtail hung down over her right breast. Her face, all bony and hollow, holding neither softness nor evil, was covered with skin like dry clay cracked a million times, fair and heavily freckled. Five lines of purple tattooed dots curved like snakes across her forehead. With all of this, the thing I remember most was the intensity of her tiny, bloodshot eyes staring into mine as though they saw my innermost thoughts. As we studied one another, I had the strangest thought, *She knows my mother's dead.*

Then she spoke, "Jar-my, ya mawmaw be kilt."

O my God, how does thing know? I couldn't speak, just nodded.

"Ya be da blackun's baabee."

"Ah...Ah...Uh huh."

"Me's Maw-ree, I's teech ya mawmaw fo dat blackun cum."

Her eyes closed, the lines on her forehead moved slightly as the skin and muscles of her face tightened, then relaxed with something like a smile that flickered and was gone.

"Ya cum out an we go."

As I crawled out of the log a crow flew down and lit on her shoulder. She nodded to it, "Jar-my, dis be Baka, me frien, he tell me ya be in da log."

She lifted a walking cane lying on the ground beside her—a sapling with a vine coiled tightly around it that had been carved as a rattlesnake. Gripping it tightly, she pushed herself to her feet. From her shoulder hung a leather bag with fringe on its bottom. She turned and pointed down the gorge with the cane.

"Ya cum wid me. Dey dis way."

She hurried off, moving as easily as a young girl over the stones. "Ya cum fas," she said over her shoulder and before I'd crawled out of the log, she disappeared around a windfall.

If it hadn't been for Maw-ree finding me I don't know what might have happened. When she told me to follow her, she moved so fast I was soon left behind and since there was no trail, I wasn't sure what direction she had gone. Then, from the far side of a laurel hell thick as a wall, there came a high, thin whistle, then a raspy shout, "Jar-my, cum dis way. Call on ye bell-eee!"

"Wha'd you say," I shouted.

"Call...call on ye bell-ee"

"Did you say crawl?"

"Ya...ya."

I got on my hands and knees and looked beneath the laurel; there was just enough room below the intertwined branches to crawl on my stomach, pushing my haversack ahead. My shirt was in tatters by the time I was on the other side and got to my feet. Before me was an almost imperceptible footpath that led up the mountain.

"Jar-my."

She was standing a little ways above me, beside a hemlock, but I couldn't see her clearly. Her features and outline were blurred. I felt light-headed; my thinking and movements were slow, yet I kept going, pushing and pulling myself upward. She never looked back; she climbed on as though I was not there.

The farther we went, the more I fell behind. Finally, I reached the top. She was waiting there, leaning slightly forward on her walking cane. A slight breeze ruffled the feathers tied in her hair. She straightened and pointed the cane at the ground next to her. "Ya sot dar."

As I let the haversack slide off my shoulder and slumped to the ground, she opened her leather bag, took a gourd out, pulled the plug and poured water over my head and gave me a long drink. Next, she reached in the bag and got a slender dried root, stuck it in the gourd's water, held it there for a moment then pulled it out, handed it to me and said, "Ya sock on dis."

I sucked it and almost immediately felt better. She pulled me to my feet, handed her cane to me, turned around and started up the footpath, saying over her shoulder, "Cum...cum."

Though my weakness soon started to return, we moved faster, crested the ridge and within an hour were down on the floor of a valley.

The sunlight was softenin as we climbed over a rail fence and walked out into a narrow field that stretched far down the valley. Near us in the middle of the field stood a single tulip tree. Its shadow fell upon four red oxen that had stopped their grazing when we entered the field, their heads partially lowered and their horns pointed toward us. A quail called. In a moment another answered. Dogs barked at the far end of the field.

We walked side by side toward the oxen. They parted, turning their muscled bodies, keeping their horns toward us. Maw-ree quit walking when we were in the shadow of the tree and began to pivot in a circle, pointing with her cane at the fields, mountains and sky.

"Aw dim luv ya mawmaw. Dat big montin dar, an dat un, an dat un, all dim mountin, all dat sky, all dim couds, dis tree, da Inyan ston, an all dis my foot be on, all dat an Maw-ree, we luv ya mawmaw, an she be wid us...I mak er cum fer ya ta see!"

She began to spin in a circle, faster and faster, her bare feet stirring dust in the air, holding her cane straight out. The oxen moved backward and as I watched, I thought I saw another figure with long red hair and for the briefest flicker I thought it was Mama. Then a small, strong hand gripped mine.

"Cum," Maw-ree said.

We walked on down the valley toward a small hill covered with beech trees. I could barely make out the outline of a house among the trees. The light was turning gray. A dog barked, another one growled. Coming fast down the small hill and leaping over the fence into the field was a boy with two large brindle hounds, one on each side of him. He walked in long smooth strides. He was dressed in gray homespun; a Colt pistol was stuck in his belt.

"Dat un cumin der be a debil," she whispered.

As the boy came up to us, he gestured to the dogs who immediately became silent and still. He stopped an arm's length in front of us; his eyes were fixed on my face as mine were on his. To this day, I think he was the most beautiful boy I've ever seen. Slender and fair with long blonde hair spread across his shoulders, he looked like a young Viking. His face was pretty as a girl's, with full lips and long eyelashes, his movements smooth as water. But his pale, unblinking eyes caused me to take a step back; they were cold and hard. I thought, *These are the eyes of a killer, the eyes of someone who would kill you and not be troubled.*

He wore patched dove gray pants, no shirt and an unbuttoned, threadbare blue cavalry jacket and no shoes. In the crook of his right arm hung a double-barreled shotgun, stuck in his pants was a Colt pistol, a long butcher knife was in a scabbard attached to the wide leather belt around his waist.

His eyes remained fixed on mine, his head turned slightly and nodded to Maw-ree but did not speak.

"Lafe, dis be Jar-my. His mawmaw be dead. Dat giant kill er like he kill ya dada...Maw-ree go now." She turned around and walked quickly back through the oxen toward the forest. Bright specks of dust and pollen fell from her hair and clothing as she passed through the last rays of sunlight. The feathers in her hair flitted like the wings of small birds.

When she was out of sight, Lafe raised the shotgun, rested the barrels on his shoulder and spoke with a voice that was soft as silk and without emotion, "That old woman's sumpun else...Did ya know she sleeps with tha Devil? She can't talk worth shit, no tellin what she's named bout me. So ya mama got kilt, huh? My daddy an brother both got kilt durin tha war. I knew yore mama an met yore daddy onst...so that makes you bout half nigger don't hit?" He pointed to the mountains, "All this hyar'll be mine one day...all of Lost Cove ul be Lafayette Washinton Pearson's...Now, by God, tell me why yer here!"

At that moment, nothing was left in me. I had made it; I was safe. I began to cry. I tried to speak, but no words came out. I began to sob and shake so hard I couldn't stop.

A hard blow struck my chest, shoving me backward as Lafe shrieked, "Shet that snivelin up. I axed ya why yer here. Ya better name it to me or I'll sic these hyar dogs on ya."

I stopped crying and wiped my face with my blood-crusted hands. The last things I remember were the hounds standing motionless, the sweet smell of the oxen and my voice answering from far away, "Mama was hung in a tree and I burned her all up." And I felt myself falling.

Yes, Lafe was right, I am part nigger. And, yes, he was a killer.

December 1943

Lafe told me that after I fainted, he dragged me to the house. I slept for two days.

Two sounds woke me: the louder, a high moaning that rose and fell without stopping; the other, a child singing softly.

> "Sleep my child an peace attend thee
> All through tha night;
> Guardyun angels God'll len thee,
> All through tha night,
> Soft tha drowsy hours are sleepin,
> Hill an vale in slumber sleepin,
> I my lovin vigil keepin,
> All through tha night."

I was clean and wearing fresh clothing and lying on a straw-filled tick in a room with log walls and a low-beamed ceiling. On the walls hung painted deerskins with scenes of dark green mountains and golden valleys filled with strange beasts. I could barely see them in the dim light of the room. Across the top of each painting, a great white angel spread its wings over the mountains and valleys; small red and white pictographs of skeletons of animals and birds were scattered over the landscape.

The air smelled of lye soap, ashes and piss. I was weak and hurt all over. I raised up on my elbows and looked around the room. The one window faced out onto a deep porch and a yard with large beech trees. Next to the bed was a wide stone fireplace; on the log mantel were stone statues of animals and several large ceremonial axes chipped from flint. On the far side of the fireplace stood two split-bottom chairs, beside them sat a large storage chest. Dresses and coats of all sizes hung from wall pegs above the chest. Three strides beyond the foot of the bed, the only door to the room was partly ajar. Through the opening, a slant of light from the dogtrot fell across a baby crib that rocked slowly back and forth. As I stared at the crib, the rocking and moaning and humming stopped. Then, from behind the crib, a young girl with long dark brown hair, dark eyes and freckles stood up.

This was the first time I saw Lillie Jane who was only ten years old and the baby of the family.

We stared at one another. Neither spoke. She studied me. She wasn't afraid. Then she reached down into the crib and lifted something out that was as small and white as a lamb. It had thin, almost white hair that hung from its large head like wisps of torn spiders' webs. The head jerked as it was lifted upward and it began to moan with a sound that wasn't of pain, but in a manner that made me think it was singing.

"We call her Angel cause Mama says God sent her. Her an Lafe aire twins. My name's Lillie Jane; what's yores?"

At that moment, the door opened. Standing in the doorway was a tall rawboned, barefooted woman with a wide-brimmed, beat-up straw hat crammed down on her head. A short-stemmed clay pipe was clamped tight between her toothless gums. She was holding a sedge broom. The skin on her face and neck was as leathery and dark as a piece of jerky. Her large hands were bony and gnarled with veins and tendons that stood out like ropes. The creases at the corners of her deep-set eyes moved ever so little as she squinted at me. She was the toughest looking woman I had ever seen.

Then—and I smile as I remember it—there was a swirl of motion and noise. Bursting into the room and around us came three girls larger than Lillie. They were all laughing and talking at the same time as they rushed over to Lillie hollering, "Lemme hold her! Lemme hold her! Lemme hold her!" Five whimpering hounds ran in and out between their legs. Behind them came a black nanny goat with a tinkling bell around her neck and hoofs clicking on the wide floorboards. Above the racket, the rawboned woman's raspy voice shouted, "Git—Git—Git!" She swung the broom at the hounds, hit one, it yelped and ran for the door; she swung at the others, missed as they fled; and with every "Git!" a stream of smoke puffed upward from the pipe that never shifted in her mouth.

Such was my introduction to the Pearsons and to Nanny, my second mother.

Except for Angel, the other sisters were peas in a pod: disheveled, half-wild looking, long-legged, dark haired, terribly, terribly loud mountain girls. Their whispers were shouts; their silence when they were together was only a breath; words and laughter flew from their mouths like birds. They were filled with fun and afraid of nothing: snakes, storms or ghosts. The mountains and the valley was their home; all they could see was theirs and on this, my first day in Lost Cove, they took me in as one of them.

None were like Lafe. It was as though he was not a part of them. Only once, and that was way later, did Nanny talk about him to me. We were sitting alone on the porch, at the opening to the dogtrot. It was a hot day but there was always a cooling movement of air through the dogtrot even on the hottest of days. A few deer flies flitted over the hounds stretched out asleep at our feet. Nanny took the pipe from her mouth, tapped the ashes out, holding it by the bowl; she pointed at the front yard with the pipe stem and began to talk so low I could barely hear her.

"This hill this house sits on is a sacred place; them beech trees out thar wur worshipped by tha Injuns. When I wus little, some Injuns come hyar from far off ta see tha trees an my daddy let em camp nar tha spring. They staid fer three days, singin an prayin in thar way ta tha spirits they say wur hyar. Daddy let em dig a hole out thar mong tha trees so's they could leave something fer tha spirits. They put in some yars of corn and baccy twists an a small carvin of a deer an a rabbit an then they filled it in. Fore they'uns left they give my mother a stone thang of a woman on her knees prayin; it's in thar on tha mantel with all them other Injun thangs we've found in tha Cove."

She stopped talking for a moment as one of the dogs began to whimper and jerk its back legs. She nudged it with her foot and it stopped, then she went on, "Jeremy, I guess ye can tell sumpun's bad wrong with Lafe. He wus marked hard by all tha ferful things he saw when he wus a chile."

She reached out and barely touched my hand with the tips of her fingers. "I prayed an prayed fer tha Lord ta heal im, but He ain't done hit...an thars times hit's hard to bare up under hit...an last night hit come ta my mind that since yer mama wus a healer maybe tha Lord sent you'uns hyar ta do sumpun ta hep im."

I didn't know what she was talking about—about me being sent by the Lord—but her whispering about Lafe and me helping him made me nervous. Any fool could see Lafe was strange, but the fear in her voice as she talked about him made me wonder even more if he was dangerous. And there I was sleeping beside him in the loft every night.

"Since he saw his daddy an brother git kilt he's turned differnt; thar's nairy a bit of joy in im. A yar ago a demon come in im after he cut hisself all up fer Angel. When hit nairy changed her a bit, that's when tha demon got in him. Now he acts like he ain't got a bit of carin in im, he won't even look at Angel, an if we'uns go ta tech im he pulls away. He even made a fist at me tha other day an had a look in his eye like he'd hit me if I laid a hand on im. If ya speak ta im he jist grunts or acts like he don't hear ye. His eyes don't even seem ta be alive. Some nights, fore you'uns come, I heerd him up thar in tha loft talkin an laughin an now an then he'd holler out a blackguard. Thar's times when he'll growl an his voice'll change, it'll go down deep inside im like someone else is thar."

She stopped. Her rough, sun-darkened hands were twisting and turning the pipe; more ashes had come out and dirtied her white apron. Her eyes were looking straight out toward the beech trees but I could tell they were seeing something that wasn't there. She took a deep breath and continued.

"He hardly hits a lick round hyar anymore, jest gits his gun an em two big ole dogs an sometimes the red'uns too an takes off inta tha mountain an ul be gone fer days an when he comes back an he's kilt somethin thar's dried blood on his face. When he's kilt a deer or a bar he'll lay a big hunk of meat on tha table an ul start inta actin out how he kilt hit, makin tha dogs' an tha animal's sounds an movements an he'll be killin hit an makin dyin sounds an pull that long knife of his out an act out cuttin hit's throat like hit wus lyin right thar on tha floor, an he'll dip his fingers inta hit an wipe his face all over. His eyes git all big and shiny an when he's done he'll look at us like he's expectin us ta clap or somethin. Then his eyes ul go dead agin an he'll go up ta tha loft an fall asleep."

She stopped talking. A fly had lit on her left forearm; it rose, lit again and began walking on her arm. Her hands slowly released the pipe onto her lap. I could see her eyes move from their far away stare down to the fly. It flew up again and just as it lit on her forearm her right hand flashed out and struck it. She looked at the smear for a second, lifted a corner of the apron, wiped the blood away, then reached into her dress pocket, pulled a twist of tobacco out, tore a piece off and, as she began to stuff it in the bowl of the pipe, she said, "Jeremy, I'd be obliged if you'uns go inside an git me a match."

Never again did Nanny speak about her fears about Lafe. Though I had not understood much of what she had said, her words stayed with me. They were to return again and again the more I was with him over the next years, and still I never understood all she meant or what she wanted me to do.

Not until six months had passed did he begin to trust me, and gradually he let me know something of who he was and what he was capable of and one day, what he would do.

I believe if Lafe had not been there, Nanny and the girls might have turned me away when they saw the hatred inside me. But Lafe was there.

January 1944

Lafe has never left me. After all these years, there are times I conjure him up in my mind. I turn in my chair—as I have just done—and see him standing in the doorway: his beautiful face set hard, his pale eyes fixed on mine, his dogs by his side; and I hear his soft voice demandin', *'Now, by God, tell me why yer here!'* And for a moment, I tense, just as I did long ago, then his face breaks into a grin and he laughs, *'Hot damn, Jerimiah, les go huntin.'*

There were times I thought he was not human; but as I look back it strikes me now as rather odd that with all of his strangeness, I can't remember ever thinking he was totally crazy or possessed. Yet, I never completely got over taking care with my words and actions when I was with him. While he sometimes frightened me with his abrupt manner—which did not suffer opposition—I was at the same time in awe of his independence, his brilliance in the forest and his harsh honesty, all of which enthralled me to the point of my wanting to be like him.

When we were in the woods he might throw his arm up to stop. Except for the flaring of his nostrils he would stand still as a stone. His whole being would be fixed on something ahead. His eyes would dart back and forth; he would sniff the air like an animal; and the tip of his tongue would come out and start to twitch up and down. If it had been possible, his ears would have twisted and turned like a deer's.

And there was something else, it wasn't until years later I knew what it was: Far beneath all the oddness and harshness, Lafe was still a little boy who had seen a great horror, a horror that had filled him with a terror that helped him kill. In my life I have been with all kinds of people. From them I have learned that Lafe, like me, was not so different than all of us. All of us have been wonderfully, awfully created so that good and evil exists in each of us—yet some, like Lafe, are different: While they see everything everyone else sees, their thoughts are sometimes not like ours.

* * * * *

During that first summer and early fall, I worked the farm with Nanny and the girls; Lafe was usually hunting or as he might grunt, "I'm gone wanderin." Occasionally, he would take everyone but me with him to rob a beehive or net fish in Crow Creek. Only twice did he take me; both times it was more an order than a request to go with him to help carry a particularly heavy deer back that he had killed. And both times as he walked ahead of me I heard him whispering and cursing, but I couldn't understand a word he said, if they were words.

We slept on corn shuck ticks in the loft. Thank the Lord we had separate beds. The eave of the roof was not more than three feet from my face. When it rained, the steady patter was better than music to sleep to. Rain or not, I slept like a log. But Lafe didn't. Almost once a week he had a nightmare that would wake me: There would be a loud rustling of the corn shucks as he thrashed his arms and legs; sometimes he would be grinding his teeth and then start to whimper, "Stop, Stop, Stop." And then, almost as it started it might end, yet there were times it went on and on, until I would get up and light a candle but that scared me too, as I was afraid if I woke him he might attack me. In the candlelight I could see his eyes were open and filled with terror. He might be staring right at me but not seeing me; he was seeing something awful in his mind. I never spoke to him and never got near enough to touch him, much less try to shake him awake. After a time his eyes would close and he would be asleep, and I would blow out the candle and get back in bed and try to go back to sleep, still wondering, *What in the hell is the matter with him?*

Then one night in the loft, after I had been living in the Cove for six months, Lafe asked a question that was to lead to our becoming closer than brothers. He never explained why he asked it.

I'd just blown the candle out when he asked, "How'd yer mama die?"

In an instant, I was reliving that night. I sat up and wanted to run. I couldn't speak.

He asked again, "How'd yer mama die?"

"What...what did you say?" I whispered.

"How'd yer mama die?"

My mouth opened but nothing came out.

And then the words poured from me and they did not stop until there were no more. By the time I finished, I'd told him everything that had happened to Mama and me the night she was killed; I told him how I found her, what she looked like when I got her down from the tree, how I cleaned her and dressed her and set her on fire. I didn't cry, I didn't feel sad or frightened, not even angry. As I talked I saw it all again: the torches, the heron, Katey, the ants, Mama in the tree, the sun in her hair, her body stretched out with her eyes closed, her hands crossed; I heard the pounding hoofbeats as the killers galloped around the house; I heard John Gaunt calling me and Lucy Taggert shouting for him to come. When I stopped talking it was quiet for a long time.

Then, in a voice like a child's, Lafe began telling how his father and brother had died. "I warn't but four an I member hit all...Queenie smelt em first, she set to runnin back an forth beside me in tha wagon bed behind tha mules, then she went ta barkin an growlin at a bunch of horsemen who weren't hardly makin a sound as they came out of tha woods. Daddy an Brother didn't see or hyar em at first fer tha loud choppin of thar axes. But when tha horsemen rode right up round us, Daddy an Brother stopped choppin. Thar was a giant on one of tha horses an he come up ta tha wagon right next ta me. I commenced ta shiverin, specially when he looked down an smiled through all that beard an hair. That skeered me so I thought I'd pretend ta be daid an, he'd think hit an, go away. But he didn't. He reached down an hitched me up out of tha wagon an spread legged me on his shoulders where he got me so I could see Daddy an Brother an all tha other'n with him. An when I seed em I didn't call em or cry cause I wus still daid.

"Nair one hep me, tha Lord didn't even come thar an, a time later, I thought maybe He wus daid too. Tha giant's hair stank an he'd fetched my legs down so hard he hurt me twixt em. Two men, jest alikes, were beatin on Daddy an Brother while tha others held em; then they started ta cut on em an Daddy was cussin an Brother had nastied hisself. An Queenie jumped from tha wagon an bit tha giant's arm an he grabbed her an squeezed her an twisted her head an threw her on tha ground, an she didn't move again. Tha mules' eyes had got big but they didn't move or make a sound; I guess they's pretendin ta be daid too.

"Then tha giant lifted me round in front of im an kissed me full on tha mouth an set me easy back in tha wagon an hollered at tha jest alikes, 'Hubert, you an Sam can get thair hair now an finish hit.'

"An though my eyes be daid they seen Daddy an Brother's skin an hair cut off thair heads, an tha jest alikes bring tha hairs over an tie em to tha reins of tha giant's horse an then they put ropes round Daddy an Brother's necks an pulled em way high up in a tree.

"I was gone away daid fer a time fore I seed my mama an sisters comin. Thair eyes looked all scairt lookin up in tha tree an at me, but I weren't scairt cause I's daid an I hain't aire been scairt again."

He did not speak for a good bit, then in his own voice he said, "Em sumbitches'll come up hyaire one day an if they do we'uns'll kill em, an if they don't come we'uns'll go down in tha valley an kill em."

"Yeh," I said.

"We'uns'll kill em."

"Yeh."

"Killin ain't hard."

"That's good."

"I'll lairn ye how."

"Yeh, we'll kill em."

"Sen them sumbitches to hell."

"Yeh."

He was quiet for a while. I thought he was asleep, then he spoke so softly I could barely hear him, "You'uns swar ta hep me?

"Uh huh."

"Shit, yer still a kid an don't know nairy a thang bout killin...but by God I'll turn ya inta a killer!" There was another silence, then, "Heed me now, I'm tellin ya, if ya speak hit once I'll kill ya...ya understand?"

"Uh huh."

He did not speak again. I lay there in the dark a long time thinking about Mama and about that night...and I prayed, "Dear God help us kill them." Then I went to sleep.

The next morning Lafe hit my shoulder and said, "Git up an git dressed an come on." I did as he ordered, put my clothes and boots on and followed him down the ladder. "Git some biscuits an ham," he said and without a word to Nanny who was fixing breakfast, he went outside. I shrugged when she asked where we were going and got the biscuits and ham and went out and closed the door behind me.

He was waiting on the dogtrot. His face was grim in the dim light. "I want ya ta hyaire me now for we leave. Don't ya aire say a thing bout what I'm gonna show ya, for if ya do I'll hurt ya...an don't ask me nairy a question bout hit. Just keep yer mouth shet!" With that he turned and we walked rapidly down the footpath through the last of the early morning mist, passed the barn and turned left onto the old trail and went up the slope to The Spur. We ate as we walked.

By the time we reached the top, the mist was gone. He stopped and looked back down the trail from where we had come; seeing no one, he slipped off the left side of the trail and pushed through the bushes and vines, still moving quickly though now there was no path. I had no idea where we were. Nearby, a grouse's warning sounded, 'Chit chit chit chit'. Just as I was beginning to wonder if he was taking me somewhere no one knew about because he was going to do something to me, we came out of the woods into a small stony clearing; on the left was a sheer drop off; on the right, a cluster of boulders and scraggly trees.

Lafe stopped. He was standing in front of a medium-sized oak. He didn't turn around or look at me. He said nothing. Cautiously, I stepped to the edge of the drop-off and looked down. Two hundred feet below was the Big Sink. When I looked back at Lafe he was walking slowly around the tree making sounds and words deep in his throat, "Tutsihusi Tutsihusi Tutsihusi Die Die Die!" As he chanted, he stared upward at the tree. I stepped closer and looked up. There, just above me was a long limb tied crossways with leather straps to the trunk; from the limb hung carcasses, skulls, skins and feathers of dead animals and birds; below these, others were nailed to the trunk. After six circles, he turned from the tree and started walking back through the woods, the way we had come.

A week later, I killed my first deer. As we knelt beside her Lafe put both of his hands on her body, closed his eyes and said something that sounded like another language. He pulled his knife out, cut her throat and let the hot blood spill over his hands. He lifted them, turned to me and rubbed the blood on my face and in my hair. "Now ya be baptized in tha name of tha one who loves killers." With that he sliced her stomach open, reached inside, cut her heart out and handed it to me. "Eat hit! Eat ever speck of hit!"

February 1944

For the better part of the next four years Lafe taught me everything he knew about killing, from wringing chicken necks to killing hogs with a heavy mallet and cows and deer with one shot from a rifle and turkeys and crows with throwing sticks and darts. I learned quickly. Soon, I was almost as good as he was at throwing a knife or a hatchet, and I could break the neck of a wounded doe with my knees and bare hands. In the second winter I did all of the hog killing and butchering. By then blood and death no longer bothered me.

On October 1, 1878, we killed the last bear killed in Lost Cove. We killed her beside a laurel hell at the foot of Jump Off Cliff. She was an old bear who had given birth to many cubs. She was larger than a yearling steer. Her muzzle was gray, her head covered with scars. Though old and missing two toes on her right forepaw, she was still strong and fast and ranged over three counties. During her life she had killed hundreds of sheep, hogs, calves and some of the finest hounds in the mountains. The year before, she had mauled two hunters; one died a week later.

We had the dogs with us when we found fresh signs of her at Prince Spring. The mast was heavy that year. She had clawed the leaves away to get to the chestnuts and acorns that covered the ground. Logs were torn apart as she searched for grubs. Her large prints were everywhere; the right forepaw with its missing two toes was well defined in the silt below the spring. A fresh pile of scat lay within a yard of the spring. Her scent was still strong.

The dogs were in a frenzy. They whined and yowled and pulled against their leashes to get after the bear that had been there only an hour before, but the day's light was almost gone. It was dusk dark and too late to loose them to begin the chase. The air was sharp and we were cold and hungry. We pulled the dogs to us and headed home; we would return early the next morning.

That night I dreamed of her. *She was huge and black. She was running faster than a horse straight down the valley toward me. Slobber was streaming from her jaws; her small brown eyes looked directly into mine. I couldn't move. I stood facing her as she came nearer and nearer. I could hear every breath she made, 'Huff Huff Huff Huff,' but as she was almost on me, she reared on her hind legs, high above me and reached for me with her long claws.* I screamed, and Lafe woke me; in a while I fell asleep again. This dream returned twice more long years later, once in Singapore, the night I killed a man; and then after Lillie Jane and I were married and I was unfaithful.

It was still dark and the others were asleep when Lafe and I dressed, strapped on our knives and hatchets and climbed down from the loft to the kitchen. Without a word we went outside and pissed, then came back in, got some biscuits and bacon and put them with extra shells in our belt pouches. I got the lantern, lit it, took our rifles down from the pegs beside the door and left the house.

A cold, heavy fog covered the valley floor diffusing the light of the lantern, obscuring objects. Sounds were muffled in the moist air, the first crowing of the roosters sounded far off.

The dogs knew we were coming before we left the yard. Lying on the straw in the barn stall they felt the fall of our boots on the ground; they breathed the odors of gunpowder and lead, bacon grease, dried sweat and our flesh and blood; they heard the words we spoke as we came toward them—words they knew—'rifle, bear, hunt, kill.' The seven were on their feet barking and howling as we came down the hill, crossed the barn lot and entered the hall of the barn. I hung the lantern on a nail and got the rope leashes. The heavy stall door shook with a dull clatter as the dogs leapt against it with all the force of their hard bodies. Above the clamor, Lafe shouted, "Damn ye, my babies, its brains and liver tonight fer supper," and then, "Bar Bar Bar!" and they went crazy.

I eased the stall door open; we pushed our way in among the swarming bodies and, one by one, grabbed them by the scruff of their necks and put the leashes on. When we were done, we led them out of the barn, across the lot and through the gate where we turned right onto the wagon road that led down the lower valley to Prince Spring. The rime-covered stubble and twigs crackled under our feet. The dogs' breaths wisped into the air as they panted and strained forward, pulling us along faster and faster until we were running behind them.

Soon we were among the trees where the bear had fed. The sun was just beginning to rise over the crest of the mountain. The fog was melting into slender streams that flowed near the ground; it glistened on the grass and bushes. The dogs were almost pulling me to the ground. I held the three brindles and two young redbones back as

Lafe took the two strike dogs forward to the scat. They snuffled it, then the ground around and in an instant Satan gave tongue with his deep, long yodeling cry, and immediately, Angel honored him with her clear ringing voice—and Lafe released them. They sprang away, leaping over stones and fallen limbs as they ran up the slope through the trees. Just as they were about to disappear, I released the others who screamed after them.

"Go ye devils...sic er!" Lafe hollered.

She had not gone far. Her scent was breast high and strong in the damp cold. She ran diagonally up the mountain, followed by the pack's shrill cry, a sustained chorus that did not falter. They went on and on, hour after hour. We ran after them as fast as our legs would go but soon could barely hear them. We leaped across the mountain like young goats, up and over logs and boulders then down and around bluffs and clefts, the pitch of the hounds' voices rising and falling then rising again as they topped one ridge then dropped down the far side; crossing streams and open glades, they climbed upward, and ran in and out of laurel hells, windfalls and rock slides. On and on they ran then slowly, toward noon, we came near them.

They were just above us in a thicket. Their steady, high-pitched squalling did not move. She was at bay and they were fighting her. The air was torn with the sounds of animals trying to kill one another: the snapping and popping of the bear's teeth, the rage of her unceasing roar, limbs cracking as she turned round and round to swing her claws at the encircling hounds as they barked and growled and darted in and out, biting at her.

"Climb damnhit, climb, they'uns got er!" Lafe shouted.

"Soooooooey pig!" I screamed. "Hol tha she-bitch, we're comin!"

They heard us. The pitch of their cries rose higher, urging us to hurry to help them kill the bear; rocks, dirt, sticks rained down upon us as we pulled ourselves upward on the roots and stones. Lafe was in front, stepping on my hands, kicking dirt in my face. I pushed him upward; he pulled me after him. Cut and torn we scrambled, falling, sliding, urging each other on, cursing with every breath, shouting encouragement to the dogs; holding our gun barrels up in the falling dirt, we crashed through the last of the brush and laurel into the clearing with our guns held forward ready to fire.

They were gone.

We could hear their cries and the breaking of limbs as they ran straight down the mountain.

"O my Goddamnit ta hell...look a thar," Lafe pointed.

On the ground, where the bear and dogs had just fought, lay one of the young redbones, torn and twisted and dead, the bear's teeth marks on its crushed head.

Lafe knelt beside the broken body and ran his hand gently over the torn red hair, "He were a good un." He stood and nodded toward the shrill crying of the hounds that were now running full out with the bear in their eyes. "Le's git that bitch fore she kills em all," and he took two strides and jumped into the hole where the bear had gone.

We ran down the broken trail made by the bear. The hounds' voices swept up the mountain, their cries echoed through the valley. The bear crossed the upper field and entered the trees on the far side into Little Cove. She was tired now. She was running slower but still fighting the dogs at every stride. Angel's splendid voice was a clear bell giving us strength. Our legs would not stop. They were filled with young blood and muscle as we came out onto the valley floor at a dead run; jumping stones and fence rails, we crossed the field and plunged into the woods. The bear was near. We could smell her. We could hear each hound's distinct voice as they maintained their attacks. One squalled in pain. The forest was filled with the bear's growling and popping teeth and the crashing of the thickets as they fought each other to the death.

They had stopped her and were holding her at bay. We ran faster knowing that she would begin killing the dogs and would not stop until they all were dead. The sun, the sky, trees, vines were all a blur; Lafe was several strides ahead, screaming, "Kill er, kill er!" And I could hear my voice echoing his, "Kill er! Kill er! Kill er!"

Now there was only the bear, the dogs, Lafe and me coming together.

And then, for the first time, I saw her through the trees. She was standing on her hind legs with her back to the base of a cliff. She was gigantic! Her body was twisting back and forth as she swung and bit at the dogs as they darted in and out grabbing at her with their teeth. Her jaws were opened wide slinging slobber over the dogs then snapping shut. Her body would bend forward to bite, then rear to its full height to slap at them as they relentlessly came at her from every side. Her eyes instantly fixed on us as we came out from the trees into the open with our rifles raised. And in that instant the other young hound leaped through the air and drove his teeth into her stomach and immediately she gave a roar of pain and rage and caught him with her front paws and pulled him to her and crushed his head in her jaws.

Lafe threw his rifle up and fired.

The explosion of the rifle and the roar of the bear mixed together in a deafening echo off the stone cliff. Through the smoke I saw her jerk backward, then she shook herself and fell forward and charged.

She was on Lafe instantly, knocking him to the ground and pressing him down with her forepaws. Blood gushed from her mouth and snout onto his face. Then slowly, almost imperceptibly, she lowered her head to his so that for a moment I couldn't see him.

I pushed the muzzle of my rifle into her eye and pulled the trigger. The explosive force of the bullet drove her sideways off of Lafe. She gave a great moan and tried to lift her head but was unable. I stepped over Lafe and put the muzzle against her head and shot her again and she died.

The bear's roaring and the gun's explosion filled my ears; my hands shook so hard the gun dropped to the ground. I could hardly stand; for a moment I felt I was going to faint. Lafe was covered with blood and brains and black powder. His eyes were closed. He didn't move or make a sound. The bear lay beside him, her left paw on his chest. It seemed I was not really there, that my lungs had quit breathing, that I was in a dream looking down on Lafe and the bear.

Then Lafe's right hand twitched, lifted slowly to his face and wiped the blood out of his eyes. They opened and looked into mine, then he smiled, "Well, I'll be damned, Jeremiah, we'uns gonna have brains an liver tonight," and he laughed wildly.

At the sound of his voice the dogs whined and yelped; they jumped and tumbled onto him, licking the gore from his face. Then they turned on the bear, growling and tearing at her body as Lafe grabbed and wrestled them, twisting their ears as together they rolled against the bear; his laughter rising higher and higher—suddenly he sat up, his face and voice cold and hard, "Hits time ta kill them sumbitches."

I leaned down and picked my rifle up and looked at the shattered head of the bear and knew I was ready to kill the people who had hung my mother. I knew that if I didn't kill them they would eventually kill me.

March 1944

Something has happened to me. I haven't been right for days. I can't remember what I was going to write next. I start writing and, in mid-sentence, I lose a word or write something that doesn't make any sense. I've erased it.

My mind feels like it's in a fog.

I keep losing my pipe and glasses.

I can't remember things that have just happened but I can remember long ago.

I've told about the bear.

What was it I wanted to tell?

Where is Lillie Jane? Maybe she knows. I think it was something important.

"Lillie Jane!"

She says I whisper. She's deaf. Why doesn't she come inside? She's always in her flowers. Spends more time pulling weeds than talking to me.

"Lillie Jane!"

Damnation, where is she?

I'll go out on the porch with the logbook and see if it'll come to me there.

Now. Maybe if I just keep writing it'll come.

The air smells good. It's clean and clear since it rained. I can see all the way to both ends of the valley. I can see the tulip tree old Levi left to shade the cows in the upper field. It's beautiful; the bark is smooth and silvery gray in the sun.

The bark on the trees is thicker this year; the hulls of the hickory nuts and the fur on animals are heavier. This winter will be a hard one.

Where is she...maybe at the cemetery trimming back the wisteria and trumpet vines? We take good care of the cemetery. How is it that I can remember the names of all seventeen of our people who are there and forget the name of a grandchild? There are six head stones with names that have no bodies beneath them: Africa, Isaac Vann, Joseph Vann, John O'Connor and Katherine Ann O'Connor Vann. I put them there. I wanted their names among us so they wouldn't be forgotten.

I think...I think I was going to tell something about last evening, but what was it? Maybe it happened a few months ago. All kinds of memories pass through my mind: some bits remain as they were; others reshape themselves; parts, or all, are lost. Surely, I wasn't going to write about last evening or a few months ago.

I remember seeing a mirage down the valley. It was a sticky hot day. There was a lake with a tree floating on it.

It is late afternoon. Thunder rumbles in the west; dark rain clouds are increasing; short bursts of wind stir the leaves. In awhile there will be rain.

The breeze wants me to walk before the rain comes. "Lillie Jane, I'm going for a walk." She didn't answer. I'll finish later.

I'm back inside. It's raining cats and dogs. I'm writing with the coal oil lamp turned up high so I can see clearly what I am writing. I wish it would put some light on my memory.

When I left to go walk I made Shep stay behind. He tries to herd up the deer; it scares them. He's a good stock dog, snake killer and friend.

The mountain's shadow was at the edge of the field when I reached the tulip tree. I sat in my usual spot at the base of the trunk. Its deep-furrowed bark is a little rough to lean against. Its leaves were rustling. The wind was blowing steady; it moved the long gray-green grass and yellow sedge in waves. Smoke from my pipe swirled and was gone. I love its smell.

As they do every evening, the deer leapt the fences in twos and threes and ran out into the field and began to graze; they were followed by turkeys, small flocks that moved among the deer. Though there's been no hunting here for twenty years the deer and turkeys are always alert, constantly looking about, ready to flee. Within minutes they were feeding all around.

A large doe came up to me. One cautious step at a time, she stretched her neck out for the grain I held to her in my hand. Just as her tongue extended she jerked her head high, sniffed the air and twitched her ears. Her eyes fixed directly across to the mountain above Little Cove. All the deer quit feeding and looked in the same direction. They all stood dead still, listening to something I couldn't hear above the wind. I cupped my hands behind my ears and listened.

A hard gust blew down the valley. When it passed, it was quiet for a minute. And it was at that time, from midway down Sewanee Mountain, there came the long high scream—like a woman in terror—of a panther.

In a single motion the deer and turkey were gone and the field was empty.

I pushed against the trunk and rose to my feet. When I was sure of my balance I began to walk as fast as I could across the field to the wagon road and on to the house.

Halfway there I could barely see because of the dark clouds covering the sky; lightning flashed and thunder rolled over the mountains. I paused, and as I did, the panther screamed again—this time not far behind me, just over the fence among the trees. I hurried, listening, but heard nothing but the wind and thunder. Then I was on the porch, and the rain started to fall in torrents.

It is still falling.

I never saw the panther. I will look for its tracks tomorrow.

I am certain that this happened.

There will be a hard winter this year, hopefully, not as bad as in '78.

That's what I wanted to tell about.

I was turning fifteen.

March 1944

Of all the winters in these mountains the one in 1878 was the hardest. All across the mountains, frozen limbs fell; entire trees split, breaking others as they crashed down through the forest. Day and night the sharp cracking echoed like rifle shots; the Cherokee would have called it 'The Winter of Popping Trees.' For a month the temperature never rose above freezing. The air sparkled with hoarfrost. Breath turned to ice. Wood and earth became iron. Water buckets and slop jars froze. Then came the snow. It seemed to never end. Layer upon layer covered the ground until the animals could not dig deep enough to reach grass, weeds, moss, or low-lying bushes. Deer stripped bark from trees but still they died by the hundreds; sheep and hogs died; hens and birds froze; a mother and three children died of starvation in Roark's Cove; a hunter froze to death fifty yards from the mouth of Buggytop Cave.

Like hibernating animals, people slumbered by their fireplaces and stoves, seldom removing the layers of clothing, hats, coats, scarves, shawls and gloves that covered them, moving only to keep the fires going, or to feed their animals or themselves, speaking only when necessary. Of all that was remembered of that year the one memory recalled by everyone was the quietness. Day after day silence, like the snow, settled over the mountains and valleys; those sounds that were heard were distinct and alone, carrying long distances: the bark of a fox, the cawing of a crow, the hungry lowing of a cow and, all around on the mountain slopes, the sharp popping of trees. Like an enemy bringing suffering again from the North, the winter of '78 came upon the South.

Every day the sky was covered by dark clouds. For a week, there were snow showers; they seemed to never leave. At noon, on the seventh day, it laid almost knee deep on the road that led down the mountain from Sewanee to Sherwood.

December the twenty-second was bitterly cold. Lafe and I had left the cove before light to go to Sewanee for a wagon load of supplies and a new cast iron stove. We were exhausted from loading the wagon and were headed home. I was driving three spans of oxen that pulled the weathered oak wagon. Beside me, Lafe rode slump-shouldered on a big bay mule with his army pistol stuck under his belt and a shotgun resting in the crook of his arm. His cavalry jacket was open at the collar. He wore no hat. Snowflakes fell onto his long hair. He leaned toward me over the neck of the mule.

"Fore yer even at tha turn off, I'll ketch ya up."

"Well hell, Lafe, it don't make me no never mind. I'm going on home."

"Ya damn better go on then, cause I might be more'n a bit."

"Lafe, you better be leaving Mr. Gipson's daughter alone!"

"I God, ya ain't telling me what ta do. Hell, she's sweet on me."

"Her daddy's gonna shoot you, Lafe."

"Bullshit!"

"Well you go on an getcha self killed, I'm going on home no matter."

"Well damn ya, Jeremiah, git yer ass on then!"

"Well I am."

"I'll likely ketch ya up fore ya git home."

"Well then I'm going on."

"Well shit, Jeremiah, quit yappin bout hit an git on!"

With that, Lafe yanked the mule's head around, kicked it hard in the ribs and it began to move as fast as it could through the snow back toward Sewanee.

I watched them until they disappeared in the snow, then I turned around and pulled my collar up and the brim of my broad-brimmed hat down to my eyebrows, picked the whip up and with a quick jerk of my arm cracked it over the oxen and shouted, "Hah on, damn ya!" The wagon lurched forward.

The oxen moved forward at their slow, steady pace. The wagon resumed its steady rocking motion on the heavily rutted road. For most of the way on the crest the road passed beneath a canopy of limbs bent under the weight of the snow. Broken branches and limbs littered the ground. Twice there was smoke from a cabin back in the woods. A mile on, the road started to slope downward; the oxen slowed; after two bends they approached a broad sandstone outcropping where there were few trees and where, if not for the veil of snow, a vista opened to the valley and the long rolling of the mountains that Nanny called, "The Graveyard of the Giants."

I could not keep my eyes open. The steady crunching of the iron wheels on the crusted snow, the rocking and creaking of the wagon and the hypnotic falling of the snow lulled me to sleep. My grip on the reins loosened and the oxen took their heads, their pace slowed. The road steepened. My head slumped forward and the dream came that is always waiting—even now.

The river is barely moving; its surface reflects the overhanging trees and tall cane. Just above the water a Great Blue Heron glides, the tips of its long wings almost touch the water. It slows, turns toward the bank and lights in the shallows, barely stirring the water. For a moment it does not move, then, one slow step at a time, it begins to walk; its eyes peer downward, searching the water ahead. Suddenly it stops. It does not move. It turns and looks at me, then turns back and, in a flash of light, its long beak spears down into the water.

The wagon lurched sideways in a deep rut almost throwing me from the seat. I jerked awake. I thought I was going over the side of the cliff and yanked back on the reins, grabbed the brake handle and pulled back hard and the wagon stopped.

"Well, shit!"

The oxen had come to a dead standstill in the middle of the road. The wagon was only slightly tilted in the rut. The stove and supplies were secure. My breathing slowed. I wasn't going to die. But something wasn't right. I looked all the way around and listened carefully. I saw nothing. The snow made a faint swishing sound as it blew across the ground and, now and then, one of the oxen blew hard through its nostrils. Except for these sounds and the cracking of a limb far below, I heard nothing.

Still, I didn't feel right about something. *Where'n hell is Lafe! He should have stayed.* But sure as hell if he had been there, he'd sneered and told me to quit acting like a 'Nancy Boy'.

A slight jolt went through the wagon. The oxen were stomping their hoofs, restless to get home to the dry barn and to hay and water. They wanted to move. The uneasy feeling left, my mind cleared, I released the brake, hollered, "Git on!" and cracked the whip. The oxen strained hard against their yokes, the wagon jerked out of the rut and moved forward.

I slapped my face, stomped my feet to stay awake and shouted, "Lord God Almighty, get me off this damn mountain, and damn Lafe! Nanny's going to have a fit if he aint with me...and damnit all to hell I'm starving!"

Coming off that mountain in that kind of weather with such a heavy load was dangerous. My left hand kept a firm grip on the reins, my right on the brake and both feet were set ready to jump. Fresh snow softened the sound of the wheels. For a moment, I thought I heard something, a horse's whinny or something, maybe the wind.

I was approaching the most hazardous section of the road: a sharp horseshoe bend around the face of a high bluff that came down close to the left side of the road. Boulders were strewn along its base, compressing the road tightly between the bluff and a stone shelf on the right that extended ten feet out into the air—Devil's Jump. From its outer edge there was a sheer drop of three hundred feet. People had fallen from there; some had jumped.

I pulled back hard on the left reins; slowly the first span pivoted around the boulders, followed by the second, then the third, each span easing forward one step at a time until the wagon was around the lower side of the bend where the road widened and straightened.

They were waiting there blocking the road, like identical iron statues: two riders, dressed in black, sitting on matching grays; coat collars, hats and scarves covered their faces except their eyes. Little mounds of snow lay on their hats and shoulders and on the manes and withers of the horses; the breaths of the men and horses and oxen made clouds in the air. Both riders held lever-action rifles across the pommels of their saddles.

Snow swept in bursts over the road, swirling upward, blurring my vision. A gust came. For an instant the snow cleared. Behind the riders stood a team of matched blacks, a buggy and a giant of a man holding the reins; beside him sat a small figure covered by a hood and cloak; both were dressed in black.

My first thought was, *why in hell are these people sitting out here in this freezing cold and blocking the way?* But immediately with the thought there was a sharp tightness in my chest. It caught my breath and I reached quickly down between my legs for the shotgun. It wasn't there! I felt along the floorboard. Nothing! *'Damn you Lafe, you took it. Where is he?'*

'Je'miah, whah ah ya? Yo mama wants ya ta come on back in now.'

John Gaunt, Confederate guerilla leader, High Sheriff of Franklin County, Grand Dragon of the Ku Klux Klan, killer of more than thirty-seven men and women had finally found me. He held the reins of the blacks in his massive hands; beside him his sister, Lucy Taggert, The Captain's widow; her twin sons, the iron statues, astride the grays. They were all murderers of innocent people; they were the killers of Lafe's father and brother and my mother.

No one spoke. One of the grays began to paw the ground, spraying dirt upon the whiteness. The rider cursed and yanked back on the reins, the horse stopped and stood as still as the one that had never moved.

A tongue clicked; the team and buggy moved forward; the grays stepped sideways. The blacks passed between them, stopping when their nostrils were almost touching those of the oxen, the breaths of the horses and oxen mixing in the air.

Lucy Taggert stood up. Though in her sixties there was nothing of oldness in her movement. She turned and looked behind the buggy seat then turned back facing me. She was as tall as her brother and straight as a ramrod, her face was covered by her hood. She lifted her skirt and stepped down onto the road. Her black high-topped shoes sank above their tops into the snow. As she walked forward her right hand slid along the back of the horse nearest her and then along the backs of the oxen until she was standing beside the wagon.

With both hands she pulled her hood back and looked up at me. Her steel-gray hair was drawn tightly back into a bun. Her face was finely chiseled, the flesh smooth and white as porcelain seemed to barely cover her skull. Her lips were full and pink as a young woman's. Her neck was long and straight as a gazelle's. She was beautiful and sensual. She was smiling at me. I did not know what to do or say. I could not take my eyes off of her intelligent ash-colored eyes that stared and stared into mine; then they began to change and the smile faded and hardened into a cold sadness.

"Jeremiah, we know all about what you and Lafe have been planning...but you're just boys...just boys. Take

my hand now and I'll help you down." Her voice seemed
so far away I could not understand what she was saying. I
could not move or speak. A small snowflake—it was tiny—
fell on her left eye and it blinked. Everything was close up
and far away all at the same time: the twins dismounting
from their horses in smooth effortless motions with their
rifle barrels pointing upward; John Gaunt rearing up to
stand on his feet like the bear, his weight tilting the buggy
as he eased down to the road and as he did, he reached
behind the buggy seat and lifted something out, then
lumbered toward me. Hanging from him like a skin, his
long black overcoat dragged across the snow, his quick
breaths mixing with those of the animals. An arm's length
behind his sister, he stopped and spoke every word
clearly, so I would hear each one, "Here, Lucy, here it
is." And he held out an axe.

She looked over her shoulder and nodded to her
brother but did not reach for the axe. She turned back to
me, "I told you to get down." She raised her hands to me.

As in a dream, I eased down to her like a child to his
mother. Her hands gently holding mine, slid up my arms
to my shoulders, her eyes never looking away, her lips
pursed as though she would kiss me. Her breath smelled
of fresh mint. I thought she was going to embrace me but
she gripped my shoulders and turned me around and
pushed me forward toward the stone shelf.

The two lever-action rifles slid and clicked. I glanced
back over my shoulder. The two grays were tied to the
back of the buggy; the twins were standing to the left of
their uncle with their rifles pointed at me. Their faces
were uncovered; they were identical: sharp boned, thin
lipped, deep set eyes, with bodies lean and straight as

their mother's, their hands like hers were small as young boys', but they were not as tall as she, nor as splendid.

As we passed her brother, her left hand dropped from my shoulder, as she whispered, "Give it to me."

She pushed me on across the road. My feet shuffled as an old man's through the snow. I could not lift them to step up on the stone shelf I was so weak with fear. I stumbled and would have fallen if she had not grabbed my coat and held me upright. She shoved me forward and stepped up behind me and pressed me onward until I was only a few feet from the edge.

"Stop!" she said.

I looked out toward the valley, trying to see through the snow, trying to see a wisp of smoke where Nanny was waiting. There was nothing beyond the ledge but falling snow.

"Jeremiah, take off your hat,"

As I grasped the brim, my hand shook so hard, I dropped the hat and a gust of wind whirled it over the side of the cliff into the air.

"Get down on your knees."

And it was then, as I started to kneel, I saw my mother standing out in the air, away from the cliff. Through the wind, I heard her voice, *Jeremiah, fight em!* and in that instant my fear was gone.

In one smooth continuing motion, my right hand slid downward so fast it did not seem to move, I could feel my fingers, tendons, muscles, flesh, all of my hand grow long; my fingers stretched down into my boot and closed around the handle of a knife and drew it out and with all of my might I sprang halfway up, turning as I rose until I was facing her and without a sound, I shoved the long steel blade through her cloak and dress and underclothes, through her flesh into her stomach, all the way to the handle. She stiffened and rose up on her toes. Her mouth opened wide, "Oh sweet Jesus," she cried, her blood spilled out onto my hand and wrist. With two quick twists the blade sliced back and forth inside her. I pushed harder and upward. "Uhhh...eeeesssee!" She grunted and squealed like an animal as I held her upright, then she slowly slumped down against me, her head on my shoulder, her body forcing me down, buckling my knees and we fell together into the snow; she sprawled across me, jerking and kicking, her face almost touching mine. I smelled the mint on her breath and saw the twitching of her lips. "Please stop, it hurts," she whispered. Her eyes were surprised; there was still something like sadness in them, and the beginning of emptiness.

May God forgive me, I shoved the knife upward as high as it would go then down. Blood gushed from her mouth and she died.

And Hell came.

Gunfire exploded, "KA POW - KA POW - KA POW!" One of the twins shrieked, "O God, he's killin Mama...O God, O God!"

"Shoot im! Shoot im!" shouted the other twin. "KA POW - KA POW!" Bullets thudded into Lucy Taggert and the snow and above us in the air. "THU - THU - THU- ffft - ffft."

"KILL IM, BOYS, KILL IM!" roared John Gaunt.

There were sharp reports of a pistol, "CRRRACK - CRRRACK - CRRACK!" A horse screamed, trace chains rattled, oxen bellowed, and then above it all I heard Lafe's high-pitched cry, "Hyarrrs killin fer all ye sons-uv- bitches!" The shotgun boomed, "BAMMM!" "Gawddamn all yer souls ta hell...I'll kill ever one of ye!" "BAMMM!" "Die ye son uv a bitch...Die!"

"O, God, I'm dead." A twin, spitting blood stumbled over his mother's body and fell forward over the edge of the cliff.

The gunfire stopped. There was silence; then one of the blacks gave a long deep moan and fell hard onto the road.

I shoved the old woman's body off to my side, rolled over on my stomach and reached for the axe. Raising my head barely over her body, I couldn't see anyone; I got up on one knee and still could see no one. Slowly I stood. For an instant I almost laid back down; blood was everywhere, its smell was mixed with sulfur and shit; two strides in front of me, Sam Taggert lay face down, his legs in the road, his upper body bent forward onto the shelf, his arms extended ahead, his rifle lying just beyond his outstretched hands.

The other black was shaking and kicking, blood spewing from its nostrils, its eyes were large and frantic as it tried to break loose from the harness. The one on its side was tossing its head up, sweeping blood and snow into the air as it tried to rise but could not, its head fell back down, it moaned in agony. The twins' horses were gone. The eyes of the oxen rolled; from their mouths came huffing sounds and mists, but they did not move.

"Pop—Pop," two soft pistol shots.

I laid the axe down, grabbed the rifle, levered a shell into the chamber, cocked the hammer and knelt on one knee. I looked beyond the wagon and the buggy but did not see Lafe or the Sheriff.

"Lafe...Lafe, its Jeremiah...Lafe!"

There was no answer; the snowflakes were smaller now; the steady wind had fallen off, now there were only gusts. I could see no one.

"Goddamnit, Lafe, answer me!"

The black's dying moans were fainter. The wounded black stood with its head down; long strings of blood hung from its nostrils, drops fell into the snow making small red holes.

"Damnit, Lafe, answer me!"

A spiral of snow swirled over the ground, covering the small red holes. Beyond the upper slope of the road a limb cracked and fell.

"Lafe! Lafe! Goddamnit Lafe, where are you?"

The horse lying on the road was dead. With the rifle in my right hand, my finger on the trigger, I bent down, picked up the axe with my left and walked across the road and looked in the buggy. On the floor was a carpetbag and blanket. There were no guns. I eased around the back of the buggy. A large set of tracks led to the boulders. I leaned the axe against a large boulder. With the rifle barrel pointing ahead, ready to fire, I stepped around the boulder.

They were both lying face up on the other side. Lafe's eyes stared at the sky; they did not turn to look at me. His mouth was partly open. A small red hole was above his right eye. A red thread ran from the hole down into his blonde hair. A second hole was in the middle of his throat. His hands held the shotgun and pistol.

I laid the rifle down and knelt beside him, leaned close to his face and looked into his eyes. They did not blink as snowflakes fell on them. There was a fleck of blood on his eye; I leaned nearer and licked it off. *Why did his eyes not turn and look at me? Where was the mist of his breath? Why did his mouth not burst forth with its crazy laughter?* I pressed my fingers against the corners of his mouth and made him smile, but it did not stay. *He could not be dead. Lafe could not die. No one could kill him. Lafe was to live and live and live forever. Why did the smile not stay on his face?* I took him by the shoulders, lifted him partway up and shook him. His head fell back, his long hair hanging almost to the snow. I shook him harder. "Goddamnit, Lafe, quit playing and get up...Goddamnit! O shit, Lafe, don't be dead...don't be dead. Please God, make him alive...please bring him back! Goddamn You! Make him alive!"

But he was gone.

Beside him lay John Gaunt, barely breathing with a full load of buckshot in his chest and stomach. It would have killed any other man outright. His coat was wide open. A dozen shot holes were in his gold vest and blue striped shirt. With each quick breath his chest jerked up and down and the dark stains spread further across the vest and shirt. Blood covered his lips.

There was no fear on his face. He did not plead for mercy or say one word of prayer to God. He lay as though at attention, his legs together, boot heels touching, toes turned out, arms at his side, his black gloved hands balled tight into fists. Lying in the middle of his chest was a double-barrel, pearl-handled derringer. His eyes watched me; in them I could see his wish to kill me.

I eased Lafe's body back to the ground, stood up and walked back to the boulder, got the axe, returned and looked down on the Sheriff. "Are you ready?" I asked.

It was then I knew the full strength of John Gaunt. He looked directly into my eyes, smiled, nodded and said, "Fuck you, you niggah bastahd!"

I spat in his face and raised the axe straight above my head and shouted, "This is for my mother and Lafe! Burn in hell, you son-of-a-bitch!" And with all my force I brought the blade down through John Gaunt's neck and into the earth.

And so died John Gaunt, killer of the guilty and of the innocent, a devil on earth—Lafe and I killed him as we had promised.

I laid the axe down and went through his pockets, got his watch and money, took two gold rings off his fingers, picked up the derringer and put everything in my coat pocket. I did the same with Sam Taggert though he had almost nothing on him. I hesitated over the body of Lucy Taggert but finally pulled her rings off and put them in my pants pocket. In the carpetbag was a half-knitted child's sweater, a roll of wool thread, knitting needles, women's underclothes, a purse and a letter.

Now the light was turning gray and the cold closed hard upon the mountain. The wind and snow were coming harder. The blood was almost covered. The dead would soon be frozen. Their bodies were turning white.

I shot the wounded horse and put Lafe's body in the back of the wagon. And then one after another, I chopped the heads of the others off and threw them, with

John Gaunt's, over the ledge. And cleaned my hands with snow.

Not far up the road, I found Lafe's mule tied to a tree. I brought it back and tied it to the rear of the wagon.

I looked around; there was nothing more to do. I climbed up on the wagon seat, cracked the whip over the oxen's backs and began the slow, winding descent down the road to the valley. And as we rode through the falling snow, I talked to Lafe: telling him the story of our bear hunt, telling him how I had killed John Gaunt, telling him that I loved him...telling him about tomorrow.

By noon we had buried Lafe beside his father and brother.

Three hours later after I'd kissed and hugged everyone, I left the valley on Lafe's mule. A haversack, filled with food, clothes, Mama's ring and comb and Bible, was tied behind the saddle. Half the money I had taken from the dead I gave to Nanny, the rest I took with me. The rings, watch and derringer were buried beneath Lafe's coffin.

Nanny knew I had to leave; if I stayed I would have eventually been connected to the killings and when they arrested me they would have hung me. And though a part of her wanted me to stay, she also knew that if I did she'd likely be charged with hiding and helping me, which could lead to her being hung beside me. So she helped me pack and get away quickly.

This time, I had to go to someplace far away where my name and face were not known and where the law would never look for me.

That place was Boston, city of Mama's brothers. Surely their love of my mother would cause them to take me in; surely they would give me work on one of their ships. Surely—or so I hoped.

As I rode up the mountain I thought how remarkable it was that death had brought me to Lost Cove and now death was taking me away. Long years later, death would bring me back.

I felt Lillie Jane's hand on my shoulder, "Come on to bed now Jeremiah, you're tired."

"Yes, I am, I'm very tired." And went with her.

When we were in bed, she was so quiet I thought she was asleep and then she said, "Have you thought what you are writing might not be good for you...that it's bringing all the awful things back and giving you nightmares?"

I didn't answer her.

"Has it crossed your mind that dwelling on the past like you do, something might slip out when the children...or God forbid, the grandchildren are here and hear it. You said you didn't want them to ever know and so I've lied for you...and I guess for both of us all these years...even after you...."

She stopped, and though it was left unsaid, I knew what she was remembering. The hurt I'd caused her was right there in her silence. I reached out to touch her but she rolled over with her back to me.

It is morning. I've just reread what I wrote yesterday. It is important for you to know that I have never blamed Lafe for what I did that day, or for what I did years later. How could I blame him, he saved my life. Lillie Jane says she still prays for him every night.

May 1944

On the train to Boston, I got Lucy Taggert's letter out of Mama's Bible and read it. When I'd finished I was so angry at its hypocrisy, I almost tore it up. But I didn't. And I'm glad I didn't. As I've grown older and faced the truth of my own self—that both good and evil have been a part of me—I have come to realize I was not that different from Lucy Taggert. I still have the letter but it is too far gone to glue in here, so I am writing down exactly what she wrote and putting the remnants into an envelope and putting it back in the Bible.

Jerusalem – Estill Springs
Tuesday, December 20th, 1878

My Dearest Daughter,

God has answered our prayers. Brother finally located Jeremiah, the Negro bastard spawn of Katherine O'Connor, the woman who caused your father to take his own life. He has been living with some people in a valley on the other side of Sewanee. As you remember, he helped his mother make her dark potions with which she bewitched your father and drove him to his death. The boys and I will spend tomorrow night at Brother's in Winchester so we can get an early start in the morning up the mountain. Then we shall see to him.

A long time has gone by since we have written one another, and I am anxious to know that God is dealing kindly with you and that all the little ones are in good health. We wish you could be here with us for Christmas, though we expect little jollification. When I get back home to Jerusalem, I will put this letter in with the other things I am sending and hope you receive it before Christmas or soon thereafter. In the box there is some muslin for you and some dark calico and thread to make the girls dresses. There is also a nice scrap of black silk that you may find a use for.

The weather here is all gloom and bitter cold. I think it may snow. If not for the hope and confidence that God gives I would be desolate and miserable. It is hard to bear as things grow worse and worse. The war brought great loss and has continued to deprive us of many things but all praise to our Father we still have our land.

The price on cotton has fallen so low the boys say we can hardly afford to make a crop next year. Your brothers work hard as there are few Negroes of any account to do work. I do not believe the Negro can be elevated to an intelligent and reliable race for their constitution is averse to responsibility. I continue to believe that God created them to be servants but in all things God's will be done. What few of ours that remain with us send their howdies, especially old Henry and our wonderful Aunt Sally.

Old age is beginning to catch up with Brother. His heart is failing but he will not cut back on eating so he is getting bigger. He is still trying to memorize all of the Psalms. He says it is good for his brain and that he likes King David. He remains the County Sheriff and is doing a good job keeping peace so we never have any trouble with the Negroes. He is still as much a terror to the ungodly as he was during the war. There are times when the boys help him out. I would not be surprised that one of them will take his place when he retires or dies from overeating. God be with him.

You will remember Elisa Capers with whom you were in school. She has lost all three of her children. Both of her precious girls died of the putrid fever last year and three months back she delivered a stillborn baby boy. She has not risen from her bed since then and her flesh has fallen away for she will not eat. I visit her every few days and try to encourage her with good memories of the past and with prayer but to no avail. Her sweet smile we all loved so is gone. Yet with all of this each time I visit she takes my hand and asks about you and the children. Her husband is like an angel as he cares for her but he looks so sad and lost. I fear she will not last out the winter.

As in all things, even those as sad as this, may the Lord's will be done.

Enough of unhappy tidings. I want you and my darling grandchildren to begin planning to come down in the spring for a visit and plan to stay a long time because we have a lot to catch up on. Tell Phillip his mother-in-law ordered him to take a rest from lawyering awhile and come with you. I miss all of you. We will have a big party and get as many of your old friends together as are still here. It will be like old times. Bring your newest hats and we will dress up and have Henry drive us everywhere in the buggy. What fun it will be.

I will finish now and get my bag packed for tomorrow. Pray for us that all goes well on the mountain. I will take this with me and I may add a bit about how our business is concluded.

Come in the spring. Love to you and Phillip and kisses for my angels.

Your affectionate mother,

P.S.   Last month your daddy and I would have been married 46 years. I still miss him so.

It is all in her letter: the opposite natures that existed within her, as they do in all of us. How can we justify our evil acts while loving and being loved and how can we continue to do good at the same time we are inflicting harm? Yet even if I had known this before I killed her it would not have stopped me. As much as I now love God, I loved my mother more. It was only later, because of Lillie Jane, that I asked for God's forgiveness. She has prayed for me for many years, she has loved me and taken care of me, and thank God she has changed me.

Though I believe Lillie Jane has saved my soul from hell, I know I remain a sinner. And while I no longer live a life of cruelty and depravity, the evil I have done I cannot forget. There is great pain in these memories that will not end until I am dead.

Part V

The Lynches and Mr. Tom

June 1944

A week after leaving Lost Cove I was in Boston. Like a long lost son come home, Mama's brothers greeted me with kisses and warmth and laughter as though they had known me and loved me all of my life. And they did know a great deal about me for, up until her death, Mama had written them long letters about our day to day life and Nanny had sent them a letter telling that Mama had died though she didn't give any of the horrible details.

I told Uncle Timothy and Uncle William everything that had happened—except for my cutting off the heads of John Gaunt and Lucy and Sam Taggert. As I spoke, their expressions were grave, at times sad, but only Uncle Timothy's face turned red with anger when I told about the killing of Mama; tears poured down his cheeks as I described how I found her and how I lowered her body from the tree and prepared it for the fire. They did not say a word while I was talking or speak for a good while after I finished.

They saved me. If not for them, I would probably have been caught and hanged. So I repeat here my prayer for them, "God bless Boston with Your love for it gave the Irish a home in America. And God bless the Lynches for giving me a home of safety and love."

Lynches were everywhere: most were common laborers and domestics, some were craftsmen and tradesmen, a few were crooks; then there were my uncles, of whom Uncle Timothy laughingly declared as he slapped me on the back, "Praise be to tha beloved

Muther of Himself, yer uncles are rich enough to barbecue a whole herd of white elephants."

They had risen from sweaty muckers to ship carpenters to being the owners of the largest merchant fleet that sailed from that great port. Now, in their fat old age, they lived with their large families in identical brick and stone mansions atop Beacon Hill.

Three days after my arrival, I was "born again" by these lovely men. Timothy proudly informed me, "Boyo, from this time forth, I'm yaire faither, as tis tha only way ta protect ye from bein found out by the law." With that he poured a glass of 'God's milk'—Kilbeggan's finest, the only whiskey he drank. He dipped his fingers in and sprinkled it over my head, "I now baptize ye, Peter Lynch after me own wondrous faither who smote the English— may their arses be covered with boils—an after our dear Lord's blessed Peter, may yaire new an glorious name save yer little brown arse." Twas a wondrous day; even better was the warmth and safety of my bed that night.

Like his father, Timothy loved his whiskey; like his father he despised politicians and those who protected them—the law. To him they were the same as the English, so the excitement of protecting me from being hung was as though he was striking a blow of revenge for his father.

He took me everywhere, telling his story over and over until it became the truth, for him and those who heard it. With one big hand on my shoulder and a brimming glassful of 'God's milk' raised high, we stood side by side in his favorite tavern as he announced loudly, "Hyaire stands me own darlin bastard boy whose daire mother—may God rest her soul—was a mulatto princess, tha daughter of a nigger queen, which makes me beautiful brown boy royalty...or if ye deny it, yerse can all fight me right hyaire an now an go ta hell!" He then turned slowly and eyed every man in the room; seeing all their glasses raised high, he shouted, "Ta Peter!"

"Ta Peter!" they shouted.

Where Timothy was full of joy and color William was all gray and black and filled with dour thoughts, which had greatly contributed to their success for he always anticipated the worst that might happen in any decision they had to make; and though occasionally they missed out on a good opportunity because of his prolonged caution, more often than not his bleak outlook on humanity avoided disaster. He prayed nightly for all who sailed the seas, especially those who sailed the ships of Lynch & Lynch.

A month after my arrival I was signed aboard the Holy Ghost as a novice seaman for a two-year voyage to China. She was a nine hundred ton, three- masted Clipper. Trim and fast, the Lynch & Lynch clippers sailed the world over, returning to Boston filled with silk and tea, spices, hides, wool, wheat, oil and occasionally, even Chinamen. I sailed in them for twenty-eight years across all the great seas of the world. In time I rose to First Mate.

The sea and the men who sailed it made me hard. Weak men did not survive long on a sailing ship. These tough, coarse men loved to sing and tell tall tales, to drink, whore and fight. They showed little sympathy for weakness; their language was filled with damnations and blasphemy; their humor was generously strung with obscenities; their tricks at times were cruel, but come gale, hurricane or the Horn, like soldiers in battle, they climbed high in the masts and stood side by side hauling in the sails, determined to save the life of their ship and the lives of one another.

In time I became like them and I loved it: the freedom of not caring for anything other than your ship and your mates and the pleasures of exploring the depths of every sin known to man and beast, with opium, laudanum, every kind of alcohol and concoction. I drank and smoked everything, whored, had visions, heard voices and sometimes believed I had special powers. If I'd believed in the Devil, I would have become him.

I killed another man; I don't remember his face or name. He was a former slave owner; for that alone I despised him. I killed him with my jackknife in an alley outside an opium den in Singapore; I killed him because he kept calling the Chinese 'niggers.'

Except for a few hours on Sunday and when we were sleeping, we were always busy: scrubbing and swabbing the deck, scraping rust from chains, painting, tarring, repairing rigging, caulking, sorting oakum, greasing and oiling, furling and unfurling sails, standing watch, mending canvas, steering—all of the hundreds of tasks that must be done to keep a sailing ship moving steadily and safely at sea.

There were many days, especially in the Pacific that had a lovely comfort to them. When the trade winds were mild, the sea was gentle and the air clear to the far-off horizon that encircled us like a crystal ring; there were nights when the brightness of the stars extended across the heavens as far as the eye could see, larger and brighter than I've ever seen them, they were near enough to scoop from the heavens with your hands.

I had just turned forty-one when Mr. Tom signed aboard in Charleston. That morning before we left port Captain Adams called the crew together on deck. After giving us some particulars about the two-year voyage we were about to head out on, he pointed to a new man. "Men, this old fellow is Tom Crossley...he's a Welshman, so likely there'll be times ye'll not always understand his talk but ye'll always love the beauty of it. He's a damn good seaman, so watch him an ye'll learn somethin...alright, Mr. Abram, give the order to loose the sails...les go to Australia!"

So it was I first met the man who would change my life. More than anyone I have ever known, Mr. Tom knew the sea and sky, the winds and sailing ships; they were his blood and breath. Though he'd lived his life on the sea since he was ten he was not like the rest of us. He wasn't crude or mean or blasphemous. I never saw him drunk. On shore leaves he usually went his own way and usually would not be seen again until it was time to reboard. But once, in Sydney, I came on him looking at books at a bookstall and he invited me to go with him to visit an old shipmate who lived at the Poor Farm outside of town. After the visit as we were walking back to the ship, tears came to his eyes as he told me about his old friend. "Dying he is, a man once strong as a herd bull he was, and beautiful his baritone voice. A better mate had no man than he...soon he'll be gathered to his fathers." The affection shown by these two old men I did not understand then, though I do now.

Sitting on the mantel above the fireplace in the room where I am writing is a photograph of the great Welsh statesman Lloyd George. I put it there because it so closely resembles Mr. Tom's strong face with its full mustache and mane of white hair and intelligent, kind eyes that were quick to smile. He had a fine tenor voice. O, what a voice it was; on calm days, when he sang his favorite hymns and the songs of his homeland they carried clear as a church bell across the ship, so beautiful and lovely we would pause with what we were doing and be carried back in our minds to times and places that had given us comfort and peace, and in these moments we would look away from one another, from the longing that showed on our faces. And sometimes, we would sing with him the one hymn that most of us knew:

> *Faith of our fathers, living still,*
> *In spite of dungeon, fire, and sword;*
> *Oh, how our hearts beat high with joy*
> *Whene'er we hear that glorious word.*
> *Faith of our fathers, holy faith!*
> *We will be true to thee til death.*

Every Sunday we all gathered on deck at noon to hear him read a few verses of scripture, then every man of us lowered his head while Mr. Tom prayed aloud for our safe return home and asked God to forgive us all of our sins for he believed as Mama did that we all need mercy, even the worst of us. We all joined with him when he said 'Amen.'

I still find comfort and thankfulness whenever I see the two of us in my mind, sitting together on the foredeck, surrounded by the long blue-green expanse of the Pacific, smoking our pipes as we mend canvas and I hear the soft rhythm of his speech as he tells me of his past: how, when he was ten, he ran away from his home in Dyserth in Northern Wales to escape working in the lead mines with the other children. And how he headed straight to the great seaport of Liverpool where he was hired as a cabin boy and went to sea never to see his home again.

The sea and ships became his home and sailors his family. He educated himself. He spoke five languages and read ancient Greek and Latin. His sea chest was filled with books; his Cicero's *Orations* and the *Origin of Species* are my favorites since he gave them to me on my forty-second birthday.

By the end of our first year at sea we were friends, and I began to tell him of my life: who my father was, how he had died, how Mama died and finally, when we were two days off the west coast of Brazil and homeward bound, I told him about the people Lafe and I had killed, even about Lucy Taggert. As I spoke of those horrors, for the first time I felt shame for what I had become, not for anything that he said for he said nothing. I think now that it was as my mother once said of people who came to her for help and told her of their hidden acts and sorrows, *When thaire confessin thaire sins tis like tha prickin of a risin with a hot needle ta get tha poison out...tis a comfort.*

And so it was with me.

As I talked about the killings, I looked down. I was afraid to see in his face what he might be thinking. I remember feeling a heavy sadness as I said, "Do you know, that old woman begged me to please stop...to stop cutting her? But I didn't, I kept on killing her...I kept on...and didn't stop until she was dead. I hated them all and wanted them dead for what they did to my mother...I was so full of hate I killed an old woman, a grandmother who loved her husband and her children and her grandchildren. I killed their mother like she had killed mine...and I was glad I had, it made me feel good...O God, Mr. Tom, I'll burn in hell for the things I've done!"

When I finished, the only sound was the slap of the waves against the bow and the creaking of the rigging. I finally looked up at him. He had stopped sewing; he was sitting with the needle and canvas in his hands, his pipe in his mouth, looking toward the horizon as though he was watching something. But there was nothing there but the sea and sky.

A warm wind from the west was pushing the sails full out; the bow rose and fell upon the waves; mist and foam sprayed over us and over the dark brown teak of the deck.

Finally, he took the pipe from his mouth and pointed up at the great white sails, "There's beautiful, they are." He turned to me and reached out with the pipe and touched my knee.

"None of us are as we would have ourselves be. Have you asked God to help you?"

"No sir, I don't know how. I've forgotten."

"No, no, Jeremiah, no you've not. The words are still there as your mother taught them to you; you just have not used them for a long time. I'll help you... Say with me the twenty-third Psalm, "The Lord is my shepherd, I shall not want...you can do it. Now, together."

He began again, "The Lord is my shepherd..." and then the words came to me as they once had so easily, and we prayed together.

"...I shall not want. He maketh me to lie down in green pastures; He leadeth me beside the still waters. He restoreth my soul; He leadeth me in the paths of righteousness for His name's sake. Yea, though I walk through the valley of the shadow of death, I will fear no evil, for Thou art with me, Thy rod and Thy staff they comfort me. Thou preparest a table before me in the presence of mine enemies, Thou anointest my head with oil, my cup runneth over. Surely goodness and mercy shall follow me all the days of my life, and I will dwell in the house of the Lord forever. Amen."

We stopped...the sounds of the ship and the sounds of the sea were the only sounds there were. Then Mr. Tom continued, "And, Father, forgive Thy child Jeremiah of his sins and give him the blessing of Thy peace." He opened his eyes and like a loving father looked at me. "Now, Jeremiah, listen you to me, there is home you must go to, your valley and your people."

Then—and this is hauntingly strange—he began to sing.

> "Sleep my child and peace attend thee
> All through the night;
> Guardian angels God will lend thee,
> All through the night,
> Soft the drowsy hours...."

And as he sang I returned in my mind to the valley and to the little girl singing to her deformed sister...and I could see Lillie Jane's freckled face and smile...and I knew....

From that moment on I was certain I could change and I knew I wanted to be like Mr. Tom, and I knew that if I tried I could be, for my mother had taught me how to be good.

Two weeks later, in a hurricane off Cape Horn, as we worked side by side furling the top-gallant sail with the snow and sleet cutting into our faces turning everything to ice, Mr. Tom slipped and lost his grip on the frozen ropes and fell from the yard arm into the sea and was gone.

There was a note in the top of his sea chest that said if anything was to happen to him the chest and everything in it was to be mine. It is sitting here by my desk, close enough that I can reach out and touch it with my hand.

Thirty-eight years have passed since he died; yet even as my memory fails, he is alive in me as fresh and near as our valley. Cicero's *Orations* lies open before me, and from its pages rises the smell of his pipe and the sea's salty air and the lilt of Wales as it carries to my ear again from across the deck of our ship that is homeward bound:

> *Faith of our fathers, holy faith!*
> *We will be true to thee till death.*

Soon after we docked in Boston I left the sea for the last time. I went straight to my uncles' offices overlooking the dock and began to tell them of my decision to return to Tennessee.

But before I could finish Uncle Timothy exploded, "Sweet Holy Muther of Jasus an a great Goddamn, what in fookin hells cum over yerse? Have yerse takin ta lunacy?" As he spoke he hurriedly splashed whiskey into a water glass and downed it in one gulp and poured another for himself and one for me, "Now, son uv me dair dead sister, drink this an drown yerse lunacy an cum ta yerse senses!" He turned to William whose eyes were closed and hands were gripped together. "That's tha way, Bruther...That's tha way...pray the good Lord's ears off til He does His job an gives the boy back his sanity!"

Uncle William reclasped his hands in prayer and raised his face to heaven and spoke with a voice that rolled strong as the sea, "Lorrrd Gawd of Hosts, reach dowwnn with Yerse mighhty hands an grabb hold of this misguided lad an shaakke tha hell from him an bring him ta his senses, fer Ye know we luv him dairly. Ahhmen!"

"Ahhmen!" echoed Timothy and took William by the arm and they turned their backs to me and began whispering. I'd half finished my whiskey when they turned around and Timothy said, " Lad, yer a man now an yerse know yer like a son ta us, so waire askin ya ta stay haire among yer blood." As he spoke he walked over to me and hugged me to him with a kiss and with tears in his eyes he stepped back, "Stay with us, lad, an we'll make ye Master of our newest clipper, Revelation."

And, yes, I did love them as they loved me; they had made me part of their families and had protected me and given me work, now they made an offering which showed their faith in me.

I suppose I was crying as much as Uncle Timothy when I shook my head, "No, sir, I can't; I must go back." And as the words came from my mouth I could see their hearts in the eyes of these kind men who loved me as much as they had loved my mother.

Words can strike like fists, so these of mine did so to Timothy whose face reddened with anger that could not accept what I had said, "Then go from haire before I strike ye!" And I left them and went up to my room and began to pack.

As I write these words the sharp sadness and guilt return for the pain I gave them by my rejection.

But they were better than I; for what they did those last hours I was among them showed the greatness of their hearts. Only a short time had passed when Timothy knocked on my door and came into the room and, in his old loving voice said, "Forgive me, Jeremiah, for I'm a stupid ole man...ye'll always be as my son an I'll love ye til I die...now rise up an wash yaire face an come down with me for we've somethin ta do."

We walked next door to William's house where all the Lynches had been hastily gathered together in the high-ceilinged parlour with Father Fitzhugh who sprinkled Holy Water over me and placed his hand on my head and prayed to God to watch over me on my journey home and as he prayed for my soul, I thought of Mr. Tom. Then he led them all in a final prayer, "Tha Lord bless you an keep you an watch over you. Amen." And with the blessing over, the whiskey and brandy were brought out. Two hours later, when it was time to return to Timothy's house, two of his sons and I supported him all the way to his bed.

At noon the next day before I left for the train station, Timothy gave me a walnut case holding a matched pair of Colt pistols, William hung a gold cross around my neck and together they handed me a money belt that held a small fortune—$25,000. I put the money belt on under my shirt and the walnut box in Mr. Tom's sea chest.

At 1:00 PM October 17, 1906, I boarded the train as Levi Thomas Crossley. It would carry me back to the South, to Nanny, and to Lost Cove. No one knew I was coming. I had not written for fourteen years.

Part VI

To Lost Cove and Lillie Jane

July 1944

It was late fall when I returned to Tennessee. The rains were good that summer. The air was crisp and breezy; the leaves on the hills south of Nashville were beginning to turn; cotton and corn had been picked; cotton stalks were dotted with their torn flecks of white; rows of corn sheaves waited to be gathered; some fields were fresh-turned earth ready for the next spring, ready for their seeds; the sky was mostly cloudy; hazy golden light lit the fields and forests. Soon after the train left Tullahoma I leaned out the window and saw the distant dark line of the mountains coming nearer and nearer; all I could think was *Home   Home   Home.*

I kept only a carpetbag with some personal items and sent my two sea chests on to the depot at Sewanee and got off at Estill Springs to visit where Mama and I had lived. As the train pulled away for Winchester, I looked around. There were a few more houses, a second church and store and a hotel sign that pointed toward the springs. A middle-aged man on a horse and an old couple in a wagon passed; they stared at me—a stranger; the person they saw was not the boy who had once lived there, but a strongly built, neatly dressed man with long hair and a large mustache. They nodded and went on by with no sign of recognition on their faces.

At first I felt excited, then as I looked across the tracks and saw the road that led to the river I began to breathe rapidly and shake so hard I thought for a moment I might fall but it passed quickly and I crossed the railroad tracks and started down the road.

Where the fences and the entrance to Jerusalem had been were overgrown with briars and bushes. I went a short ways down the lane toward the house, far enough to see that only the chimneys were still standing, then I turned and went back to the road.

Nothing remained of our cabin, the forest had returned. A briar patch covered the fairy stone. The only thing still there as it was before—though now half dead and shorn of its top and most of its once broad limbs—was the oak where I once had sat waiting for Captain Taggert to pass by on Lady and where I had found Mama hanging high above the limbs that were left. Nothing but the river was as it had been, I pushed through the growth on the bank until I stood at its edge; it seemed almost unchanged: the overhanging trees, the cane, the slow moving water and as I stood there seeing in my mind's eye all the memories of my childhood, a kingfisher flew by, followed by a pair of wood ducks and then, out of sight, I heard a deep harsh cry and around the bend came a Great Blue Heron, stroking the air with its long wings as it passed me.

I spent the night at the hotel in Winchester, signing Tom Crossley on the registration book. I had left the county as Jeremiah Vann, a lanky mountain boy with a high-pitched voice in patched clothes. I had returned dressed in my best sea clothes as Tom Crossley, a strong, self-assured, forty-two-year-old man with black hair and mustache who spoke with no special accent.

When I checked into the hotel, the young desk clerk studied me carefully. Finally he asked, "Sir, if ya'll don't mind my askin, where ya'll from?"

I looked up from the register, "No, young man, I don't mind you asking. I've come down from Boston, and before that I lived most of my life on the sea, and when I was a boy I lived in Wales."

His eyes got big, "Ya'll are pullin my leg...ya'll did'n live inside a big ole Whale, likes in tha Bible...ya'll are funnin me...ain't cha?"

I laughed, "No, no, not a whale, not a fish...Wales is a country...it's spelled W-A-L-E-S. It's across the ocean, right next to England."

"Oh yea, I think I've heard of that place, that's where Robin Hood an a famous king lived. They's tha people we beat ta get ourselves free...right?"

"You got it."

"Now, Sir, one more thing an I don't wancha ta think rude of me askin all these questions but I was born curious an I'm always wantin ta know about other folks an things...So what brings you all tha way down here ta us?"

"Well Sir, I've come to see your beautiful mountains, to breathe your good air and to visit your famous university that sits up there in the clouds."

"So ya'll goin on up ta Sewanee tomorrow?"

"You're right, young man. Now would you be so good as to give me my key and point me to my room!"

Early the next morning I hired a driver and buggy to take me to Cowan where I boarded the train for the long steep grade to Sewanee. As the train chugged its zigzag way up the mountain I was remembering hiding in the gully, covered by briars as John Gaunt and his nephews sat on their horses near me; then the long hard climb up the mountain that night. As these memories came, I felt the return of the apprehension I had had at Estill. What might be waiting on the mountain; it was there that terrible winter day that I was almost killed. For a moment I thought of jumping off the slow moving train.

Thank God I didn't.

The first thing I heard when I stepped onto the depot's platform was the University of the South's chapel bells ringing the students to morning service. I paid the depot master to hold my chests until I came to get them and walked up the main street of Sewanee. It had grown: new houses, stores and an inn lined the street: some clapboard, some crab orchard stone. The University and new church were located near one another. The old blacksmith shop and stable were still there but the store where Lafe and I had gotten Nanny's new stove was gone, now an empty lot grown over with weeds and small saplings.

Two lots away was a new store. As I passed in front, Zeke and Eli Garner came out the door and walked by me; both looked right at my face, but again there was no sign they recognized me. Other than them I saw no one else I knew.

At the far side of town I turned around and came back through and went out the west side; a short distance on I turned onto the Sherwood Road that led out to Natural Bridge, Devil's Jump and halfway down to Lost Cove and to Nanny—if she was still alive.

For a bit, there were more houses, more cleared land, but a half mile on I was beneath the tunnel of trees that I had driven the heavily loaded wagon under twenty-eight years before; though it was autumn and the trees were full of color, that terrible, white, bitter-cold winter day was there, all around me.

I don't believe in the existence of ghosts or specters or the actual return of the dead from the past, or in seeing into future times; I believe our minds fill with all kinds of things from when we were little right on up until we die, but I also believe there are times when something happens that brings the past so clearly and powerfully back into our thoughts that we feel as though we're actually reliving the past and are seeing and hearing people long dead.

As I walked the Sherwood Road, I heard the crunching of the wagon's   wheels in the snow and Lafe's laughter as he jerked the mule's head around to return to the store owner's daughter, and then only a little farther, I came to Devil's Jump, the sharp bend in the road, the stone shelf...and it all was there. I could see them, dressed in black, waiting in the middle of the road, the air freezing, the snow on the oxen's red hair, icicles hanging from their nostrils; I could see Lucy Taggert's sad eyes and the axe in her hand; I could see myself kneeling at the edge of the cliff and the blood spreading across John Gaunt's vest; I could hear every sound—explosions of gunfire, shouting, horses screaming and above it all, the voices: *Jeremiah your just a boy...please stop it hurts...Hyarrs killin...Kill im, Kill im...Lafe where are you?...you black bastahd...burn in hell you son-of-a-bitch.* I could feel the axe blade go into the earth, over and over, and the wetness of the hair as I threw the heads over the cliff. I could see Lafe's eyes open and the speck of blood on one of them and his open grave with the earth and the snow piled around it. All of it was there. None of it has ever left me.

I was near to turning back when Mr. Tom's words came again, *Now, Jeremiah, listen you to me, there is home you must go to, to your valley and your people.*

I ran, turning onto the narrow wagon road that led down into the Cove. I ran, leaping stones and fallen limbs, hearing ahead the crying of hounds running full out down the mountain, and beyond them, the shout of Lafe calling to me to hurry on, *Jeremiah, we'uns gonna have brains an liver tonight.*

And then I was down standing at the gate and rail fence at the edge of the pasture near the head of the valley. Straight across the field was where Maw-ree brought me out of the woods. From there, standing in the field, I first saw Lafe and beyond him the hill where the beech grove was and the house. The giant tulip tree was there just as it seemed to have been forever; beneath it, several brindle cows lay chewing their cuds in the shade.

Wild roses, blackberry and trumpet vines, fireweed and sunflowers grew around and over the fence; bees, butterflies, grasshoppers flew and flitted everywhere; quail and meadowlarks called from the field and fencerows, crows cawed from the woods; and all around the valley's floor rose the mountains. It was as I remembered: the colors, the scents and sounds of the long green valley.

Yes, I am home. I still see and hear things exactly as they were, the valley where God brought Levi long ago, the forest, the bluffs of the mountains, the calls of quail from the thick grass and the voice of a girl singing to her sister, the screaming cry of hounds fighting the bear, the shout of Lafe calling me on. Yes, it is as I remembered, but for those I have loved, are they still here? Are Nanny and the girls, is even one who once cared for me still here and, if they are, will they love me as they once did?

I went along the wagon road until I reached the barn where I turned off onto the footpath that went past the spring and up to the house. I stopped there, knelt down and cupped water to my mouth—*the best water on earth!* As I climbed the hill to the front yard I heard a woman singing. Her voice came through the open windows.

> "De Camptown ladies sing dis song,
> Doo-da, doo-da,
> De Camptown racetrack's five miles long,
> Oh, de doo-da day.
> Goin to run all night,
> Goin to run all day,
> I bet my money on a bob-tailed nag,
> Somebody bet on de gray...."

As I stood there listening, a black and white collie jumped up from where it was lying on the porch and rushed toward me barking.

The front door opened; Nanny and a small, stunning woman holding a raised shotgun stepped out onto the porch. The sun was shining on them. Nanny was unchanged: tall, angular, barefooted, pipe in mouth and still blunt with her words, "Wail who'r ya, an what brings ya down hyaire?" The other woman didn't speak.

Nor did I.

I stepped nearer and raised my face so they could see me clearly. Nanny's eyes squinted; she studied me carefully then broke into a toothless grin, "I God, Lillie Jane, it's Jeremiah."

Still Lillie Jane did not speak. I couldn't take my eyes off of her. She was so cute and pretty; her short dark brown hair framed an intelligent face with dark, feisty eyes and full lips; she was all feminine and strong at the same time, her bare, firm arms and legs were brown from the sun; she had a tiny, tiny waist.

In a slow, easy voice that was almost a drawl she said, "Jeremiah, is it really you?" Her eyes looked straight into mine, and from that first moment, I thought, *My God, she's glorious.*

For a long moment I said nothing, then I smiled and nodded, then I said, "Yes, it's me...you can lower that gun."

With that, she laid the shotgun down on the porch and ran down the steps toward me, "O my, it is you, Jeremiah...it's you!" And before I could raise my arms she grabbed me and kissed me full on the lips. I could feel her body tight up against mine; I pulled her tighter and opened my mouth to hers.

Til this day, I've never known, nor have I asked Lillie Jane how it was she saw goodness still in me that I'd thought had left me all those many years ago. I was afraid she would only see darkness—for it was still in me. Though the preachers say we are born in the image of God—and I will not call them liars—there is still much of me that will say, *Yes, you may be right for most, but there are some of us who are not.*

* * * * *

Only Lillie Jane and Nanny remained when I returned to the Cove. The others were gone.

Jane Anne, the oldest, married Joe O'Leary, an engineer for the Nashville, Chattanooga & St. Louis Railway. He had a great irreverent sense of humor. Every summer, their two boys stayed with us for a week or two. Both of them were killed in the Great War. They are buried with their parents in the Catholic Cemetery in Nashville.

Betty Sue married a man I never met. Luther Pullen was a young farmer from Roark's Cove. According to Lillie Jane he couldn't stand being closed in by the mountains and dreamed of growing wheat like 'an ocean of gold' on the prairies. They went to the Dakotas in 1889. They wrote one letter back from St. Louis, saying that all was well and that their wagon was loaded and they were heading out early the next morning. No one heard from them again. Six months later, two of Luther's brothers went looking for them and found nothing. The last person they thought might have seen them was an old buffalo hunter who said they may have been the people he'd passed in his wagon three days west of the river and seemed to be alright.

Patty, the third sister, became an old-maid schoolteacher in Sherwood; she lived here til she died of old age. She never married. I don't know why, when she was young she was almost as cute as Lillie Jane and fun to be with. It's a pity she didn't marry and have children; it might have helped balance her on religion. As she got older, she became a fanatic and spent all her time memorizing the Bible and going to revivals. At times, she was hard to bear when she got to condemning others and quoting scripture. It got so bad, I'd sneak away to the barn or go stay in the woods when she came to visit. During her last years, I don't think a smile crossed her face, which stayed frozen in a scowl as though she always smelled something bad—I guess it was the odor of sin and it was forever around her. We buried her several plots away from Angel and Lafe.

In the Pearson Cemetery, right behind Nathaniel's grave, is a small weathered gravestone with "Tennessee—God's Child—1859" carved on its face. I once asked Nanny about it, she said, "Twixt Patty an tha twins thar came a daid chile, fer a time hits comin that way nair crazied me, til the good Lawd sent us another un an hit lifted me up, so we named her Angel Grace."

Angel lived far longer than I had thought she would. Before she died, I came to believe as Nanny and the others did about her for though she was blind and mostly deaf, she knew everything happening around her—especially that she was loved. And you could see it in her smile, the twisting of her body and hear in her moaning that she was saying, "I love you." Though I grew to become a doubter and skeptic about religion, I never doubted that she was an Angel. God bless her!

Lafe didn't believe any of this about his sister. One night, before we fell asleep in the loft, he said, "All that stuff they go on bout Angel an God an bout her telling us thangs is a crock uv shit! Thairs been many a yair I prayed ta God ta make her right an nothin happened. When I wair ten I climbed up in tha barn loft an cut both my arms an asked Him ta take my blood—all uv hit if He wanted hit, but He had ta make her right...but He didn't do nairy to hep her. He didn't do a goddamn thang!"

Angel died two years after I first came to live with the Pearsons. The morning of the day she was to be buried, I offered to help Lafe dig her grave. For a moment I thought he was going to hit me with the pick. He didn't say a word and I let him be. As soon as she was buried he got his gun and left. He was gone for five days.

* * * * *

Three months after returning to the Cove, Lillie Jane and I married at the Episcopal Chapel in Sherwood. We married as Mr. and Mrs. Tom Crossley. We've had three sons and two daughters. The first one was a baby boy born dead. As I write this, the pain of it returns. There was a sadness in this loss that has never completely gone away. Willie came a year later. Like his mother, he is beautiful and good. He visits us twice a year. Our other son L.T. has a farm near Schochoh, Kentucky; he raises tobacco, corn and a few cattle. Grace and Fannie both married. Grace's husband Charles Sheldon is serving in the Army as a cook. Thank God he's remained in this country and not been sent to Europe or the Pacific. They have no children. Fannie married George Joseph Spain who is over the age limit to be in the military. He sells cars. He sometimes comes to the Cove to hunt. We like him. He's a go-getter and friendly and loves his family. They have two daughters, Jane and Jill, and a son, George Edward, who's the oldest; he comes to stay with us in the summer.

Nanny lived with us until she died in 1930. She lies between Nathaniel who died in 1864 and Lafe who died in 1878. What do I say of Nanny's life? It is this: She was born to suffer hardship and terrible loss but her heart never dried to bitterness; she helped runaway slaves; she loved Nathaniel and her children; she loved her deformed child equal to the others; she loved her strange, hard son Lafe; she loved my mother and me as she did her own; she loved our children; she loved...can better be said? The only answer to death is living and loving.

* * * * *

Other than one long trip to Boston to visit Lillie Jane's cousins and rare trips to Winchester and Nashville, we have seldom left these mountains. With the exception of Lillie Jane, Nanny and Aunt Sally, no one has recognized me after all these years. Now that Nanny and Aunt Sally are gone only Lillie Jane and I know what I did sixty-six years ago. Not even our children know my true identity.

Only once since my return, has Lillie Jane called me 'Jeremiah.' It was in 1918, when she almost died from influenza during the great epidemic that killed a number of our neighbors and over a half million Americans. It came on her quickly, with aches, chills and fever; in a few hours hard nausea began and by the next morning she was dehydrated and her fever had risen to 104; her skin had turned a bluish hue. I had been with her all that night and could see her getting worse. She was burning up and, now and then, she moaned and said a few unintelligible words. Her eyes were closed.

She's going to die. I laid the wet cloth down that I was using to cool her face and stood up.

"Lillie Jane, we've got to get you to the hospital."

Slowly her face turned toward me; her eyelids barely separated; she shook her head and whispered, "No."

I sat down beside her, placed my hand on hers. "Precious, we've got to go...we've got to." I got up, leaned forward, put my hands and arms under her and began to lift her.

She groaned and, for the first time since the day I returned, spoke my name, "Oh, Jeremiah...please don't...it hurts...lay me down."

I eased her down and was about to speak, when she said, "Jeremiah, please don't take me...I'll die there for sure...you take care of me."

She was so weak; for the first time ever, I saw she was afraid. None of the children were in the room.

She shook her head and mouthed, *Please.*

I didn't take her.

For three days I nursed her, doing all the things I'd learned from Mama and from seamen who nursed us at sea. And though I felt no certainty about the existence of God, I prayed day and night that He not let her die.

She recovered.

If it was God who saved her I give Him my thanks until I die, as I thank Him for making her as He did: wise in mind and heart, kind and forgiving, most of all I thank Him that she stayed with me and never stopped loving me.

She has loved this valley and these mountains her whole life. Except for the years she was in school in Winchester, she has never left. That love was not in her sisters. I think of all of the children, even Lafe. It is only Lillie Jane who loves it as old Levi did.

She was ten when her father and brother were killed; fourteen when Lafe was killed. Angel was dead. Tennesse was dead. Death was part of her life. Her sisters were married and gone. It was then, I think, that Nanny made a hard but wise decision. She saw there was something special in her last child; her curiosity for everything around her and her love of books that her teacher at the little Sherwood school lent her. She could see how her daughter's eyes lit up when she talked about her dream of becoming a teacher.

That next spring, Nanny sold the last stand of virgin timber in the Cove to pay for Lillie Jane's admission to Mary Sharpe College in Winchester. For four years she attended school there and boarded in a nearby home where she paid for her upkeep working as a maid and cook. During those years she went home only one week each year.

After graduating with honors she moved back home and was hired as the teacher at Sherwood's one room school. She bought a saddle horse and rode it back and forth to school carrying a loaded pistol in her saddlebags. Nanny said that three men wanted to marry Lillie Jane but she had turned them down with the single explanation that she wasn't ready to give up teaching and to have children.

In those days a woman with a college degree was a rarity in the mountains, even at the University. While it didn't make her uppity, her speech changed; her vocabulary and pronunciation were those of one well educated.

With all I can say about her, how can I tell you of my love for Lillie Jane? All of the badness had not left me when we married; there were times when I drank too much and there were times when I was a womanizer and lied to her. It hurt her terribly. For a while she slept with her back to me; her face was sad and she lost weight from not eating. But gradually she healed and trusted me again.

Two years later, I was unfaithful again. This time she was so enraged when she found out she struck me in the face with her fist hard enough I almost fell. I came close to losing her then. Yet she stayed; I think it was because of our children—for I was a good father to them and they loved me—and I think she still loved me. Somehow my running around and drinking slowly left and I changed and became a better man.

Our outhouse, well house, chicken house and smokehouse are all painted purple, her favorite color.

My Lord, she's feisty and as honest as the day's long! She absolutely cannot bear a lie, not even the shading of a truth. She'll immediately correct me, or our children, even a stranger if there's a hint of an intentional lie. Our grandchildren love to repeat her words to them, "You can say anything you want to as long as it's true." This, of course, they use to defend themselves when they say something that is cuttingly direct about the disagreeable traits or appearances of others.

She is five feet two inches tall, still trim and pretty, her soft dark brown hair is streaked with gray now. Her soul is filled with color, music and adventure. She is small, feminine and so soft-spoken that unless you knew her you'd never imagine her to be the best shot in the mountains with a pistol, shotgun or rifle. Long ago, the Garners nicknamed her "Dead Eye Dora."

Can you imagine that a woman like her would keep my underwear clean, much less mend my socks and shirts, milk, make butter, make buttermilk biscuits and milk gravy for me to have at supper every night and keep my one suit nice and ready for funerals and Easter Service?

And O my God, she was a good lover! Every one of our five children came right on time. Those days began going a few years back and are gone now, I guess forever.

As my mind has gotten worse, I'm more dependent on her and never want to be too far away, never farther than shouting distance. Everyday it comes on me that I just need to touch her, just to know she's there.

There's a photograph of her that was made at a Sewanee studio the week before we were married. It's one of my favorites. It sits on a dressing table in our bedroom. Her face is turned slightly away from the lens of the camera, her wavy hair is cut short, her hands are partially clasped with the fingers intertwined; her smile is radiant. Lord God, what a woman!

August 1944

A hard crack of lightning near the house woke me early this morning. Rain is coming down hard; it sounds like hail pounding on the roof. Maybe it is. Except when there's a flash of lightning, it's pitch-black outside. The coal oil lamp is bright enough for me to write. Just before I awoke I was having a dream about Lafe. I got up and came in here to write it down while I can still see and hear it.

He is hunkered down in a thicket of dense brush that grows halfway around a partially frozen pond. Behind the thicket is a scattering of trees where the forest begins, then the hills.

It is sleeting and snowing but not hard. The lightning flashes are quick. There is no wind. The sky is filled with low dark clouds; the air is the color of ashes.

Lafe is turned away, the collar of his heavy coat is turned up and an old wide-brimmed cavalry hat is pulled low down on his head. His face cannot be seen. The barrels of his shotgun are sticking up above his shoulders. He is listening to something.

For a long while, there is not a sound or movement but for the falling sleet and snow. Then through the bare black branches of the trees atop the hills, lights flash far away and there is a faint sound like the cry of running hounds coming toward the pond.

Lafe stands, puts the shotgun to his shoulder, the raised barrels point above the pond toward the hills. There are two sharp clicks of the hammers being cocked.

And in that same instant, the loud calling of geese comes through the snow from above the hills. A large flock appears; they are flying fast with their long necks extended, calling again and again to one another as they drop downward, their wings spread to glide toward the pond. There is a loud boom and the hard flapping of wings, and they are gone, and the air is thick with smoke.

God, save me from my dreams and terrors. Make Yourself known to me. Do not hide behind the face of the world You created or the voice in the Bible.

Mama once told me that everything in a dream means something about the person dreaming. Like a play, we write the script; design the set; are every character, animal, tree and cloud; every sound and word that is spoken is from part of us; we create it all in our heads; it is all about the one who dreams.

I fell asleep thinking about Mr. Tom's death in the snow and hail at the Cape and awoke from a dream about Lafe and snow. I don't know what in hell any of it means. I dream more than I used to. If I don't write them down immediately I forget them by the time I go to the bathroom. Mama, Lafe, the mountains and what happened on Elk River are in a lot of them. Mostly, I feel fear when I first wake up from a dream but it goes away soon.

The lightning and thunder are moving off to the east, the rain is breaking up; I hear the cow bellowing. I'll milk her after I get Lillie Jane's coffee.

[Following the notation of August 1944 there were two blank pages, then this final entry was made without a date. G. S.]

I have not written for a long time. I'm losing interest and can't keep my thoughts straight. It's too hard. How strange...I don't even know what day or month it is, much less the year.

I am becoming more confused about what is going on around me. Every day my memory is worse. What is so strange is I can still remember all the things Mama and Nanny told me more than seventy years ago. How is it I remember the name of Africa who taught my father to carve; and the name of William Dudley, the man my father killed; and of Lady, The Captain's horse; and of Father Fitzhugh who poured the Holy Water on my head in my Uncle William's parlour? How is it my mind still sees the heron's yellow eyes and the speck of blood on Mama's white comb that I saw when I was a boy? They are as clear to me as these words here in front of me. I hear Maw-ree's strange voice and the whirr of the fairies' wings under the moss-covered stone and the lilt of Mr. Tom's voice praying for me, praying that God will forgive me.

It is happening to me this very moment.

I see their faces and hear their voices. Nanny and the girls laughing in the other room. Lillie Jane singing.

> *Sleep my child an Peace attend thee*
> *All through tha night;*
> *Guardyun angels God'll len thee,*
> *All through tha night....*

Lafe. I hear Lafe...I hear him calling me to hurry: *Goddamnit! Jeremiah, come on.*

I'm coming...I'm coming. Lafe, you better leave that girl alone.

Ye git on, Jeremiah, I'll ketch ye up.

Well, I'm going on.

Well, I'm going on.

I need to ask Lillie something first. Have we eaten yet? Where is she? We'll have to eat good before we take the wagon up the mountain in all that snow. Damn it's cold outside! "Lillie Jane...Lillie Jane, where are you? Tell Lafe to hurry up."

O Lillie Jane, how beautiful you were that day, standing in the sun, a woman grown to loveliness from the little girl I first saw with her long dark brown hair and dark eyes singing to her crippled sister. And now you are an old woman, wrinkled and gray, and I love you now even more than that day when I returned and saw you there on the porch with the sun in your eyes, and I knew that moment I would marry you. If there is a heaven, let it be here. Let us return to this, our valley, forever.

All of our people are here.

If I am gone when you read this, Lillie Jane...I will be back soon.

I'm tired of writing.

There is no more to say.

Epilogue

by
George Spain

The year after he finished writing *Lost Cove*, Granddaddy died of a stroke while he was sitting on the porch. Nine years later, Grandmother died in an old ladies home in Nashville. They are buried side by side in the Pearson Cemetery. Granddaddy's stone originally read Levi Thomas Crossley 1864 - 1945. I went there a few months ago with a hammer and chisel and carved "Jeremiah Vann" above, and "a.k.a." in front of Levi Thomas Crossley.

My sister Jane now has the walnut box with the bone ring and comb in it. I have Annie Lynch's Bible.

We gave the sea chest to a cousin in Kentucky who loved him almost as much as I did. She keeps it in her living room as a keepsake chest.

Brad, our oldest son, has a log cabin in Williamson County where he sleeps every night in the bed that was Jeremiah and Lillie Jane's.

I have the *Lost Cove* manuscript and Mrs. Taggert's bloodstained letter. When I die they will go to the Tennessee State Library and Archives. The Lynch Bible, Jeremiah's books and the Colt pistols will go to our children.

Lost Cove was sold to the Garners in 1955. They later sold the mountains surrounding it to the University of the South and the valley floor to a gracious lady and her husband who have become my friends. They have taken our children and me there, during which time we visited the site of Levi's and the Pearsons' old house; only the chimney remains. The barn where Lafe kept his hounds still stands. The Big Sink is as wild as it was in Levi's day; Prince Spring, where the bear hunt began, still flows freely. Most of the stones in the Pearson Cemetery can still be read: Nanny's and Nathaniel's; Lillie's and Jeremiah's; Nancy Angel Pearson's, with a sleeping lamb carved on it. Some are gone. There is no stone for Lafe.

The summer of 1944 was the last summer I stayed in the Cove with my grandparents. I was eight. Though it was almost seventy years ago it is etched in my memory as if it were yesterday. With the promise that I wouldn't go into the forest or near the Big Sink, they let me roam the open areas of the valley floor on my own. Standing barefoot in the reddish dust of the wagon road, out of sight of the house, was glorious. All the tales about Levi, the Indians, of buffalo and the bear hunt filled my imagination so that I was back in time with my long rifle and tomahawk peering down at the dust for moccasin prints or pad marks of a panther. I walked the road as hunter and explorer all the way to the north end where it led back into the woods and up to Natural Bridge.

I stopped there, turned and looked down the long field that went south almost a mile before it turned east, making the L that Levi had seen from atop the bridge as a sign from God.

I took my shirt off, then my pants, and immediately I was an Indian scooping dust up, rubbing it into my skin and hair and on my face—I darkened myself so that other Indians would know I was one of them and would not kill me as a white man. Now my ears understood the voices of the birds, my nose smelled the smells of animals in the forest, my eyes saw the spirits in the air.

I began to run down the valley.

Like a deer I leaped down the road high above patches of grass and ruts and stones. I ran faster and faster; my face half-black, half-red; my tomahawk raised to kill. On and on I ran shouting my war cry, *AAAAHEEE... AAAAHEEE....*I ran and ran until I could run no more, sweating and gasping for air until I gradually became myself again. As my breath returned I began to turn in a circle looking up at the mountains and around me at the floor of the valley—all that I saw was as it should be. Even then, I knew that what was there was special and I began to say out loud, *All of this is ours...all of this is ours...all of it...all of it.*

I can close my eyes and in an instant that summer comes back: the lean hogs running half-wild through the woods; Mag and Dolly, the matched pair of bay mules, pulling the wagon steadily up the mountain; Granddaddy and I sitting side by side heading to the store in Sewanee; I hear "Mama", the milk cow, her eyes like a doe's and her milk the richest I've ever drunk, lowing every morning and evening as she wound her way from the pasture, her full bag swaying, ready to be milked; I hear the shoosh of milk in the bucket as Grandmother taught me to grip the tit with my lower three fingers and then to strip the milk down; I smell the acrid odor of the outhouse where flies and wasps darted around your head as you hurried to get off the wooden seat so as not to be stung; and I taste the air of salted meat in the smokehouse. Birds, butterflies, grasshoppers and insects were everywhere.

Thank God for memories; though some are filled with pain, many are happy, especially that final summer, sitting high up in the wagon in the hot dusty air beside my grandfather on the hard wooden seat as he brought hay from the fields. With his sleeves rolled above his elbows I could see the faded blue anchor on his left forearm; his hands loosely gripping the reins that led to the iron bits in Meg's and Dolly's mouths; their bodies pushing against leather collars as they moved together as one across the stubbled field heading for the haystacks in the pen beside the barn; and as they passed through the open gate at the corner of the field, Granddaddy calling out, 'Gee', and they would turn right onto the lane that led to the barn.

Though I now know who my grandfather was and the bad he did in life, I love him all the more for how he changed and for who he became. But even as a boy I saw there was still darkness in him. At times he was solemn and withdrawn, saying little; he was elsewhere, lost in his thoughts, unaware of us. He would close himself in his library with his books for hours or he would leave the house telling no one where he was going. All Grandmother would say was, "He's feeling poorly today, just let him be...it'll pass." But now I know it never passed.

He wrote most of *Lost Cove* in the library. The room smelled of him—tobacco twists, old pipes and old books, lye soap, King Leo Peppermint Candy, and Shep his English Shepherd companion. The candy was in a tin on the mantel, and every night after supper I would climb up in his lap and we both had a stick.

When he wasn't feeling 'poorly' he would tell me a story. It was only when I read his journal that I realized that most of them I had thought were made up, had really happened. The bear hunt, the witch with red hair, the storms at sea, fairies, Indians and slaves were all from his life and the life of his people.

My grandmother lived her life by faith and with an unshakable common sense that cut through stupidity and excessive reflection. She did her best to teach us to be good and, all in all, it worked. Though she was a strong Christian and wanted us to be, she was rarely openly critical of others; she let them alone to be what they wanted to be. But telling a lie was another thing altogether. Once, when I was seven she whipped the devil out of me for whirling her hens around in a feed sack, making them drunk, then dumping them out on the ground to watch them stagger. I accidentally broke the neck of one. When she asked me if I knew how it had happened, I lied.

"It was runnin an tripped on a rock, I guess," I told her, but as the words came from my mouth, I looked down at the dead chicken and began to cry.

She stood there and let me cry for a bit, then she asked, "George Edward, tell me the truth now...is that what really happened?"

I wiped the tears running down my cheeks and the snot dripping from my nose with my sleeve. Still looking at the dead chicken, I shook my head, "No, Ma'am."

She was quiet for what seemed an awfully long time, then she said, "Thank you for telling me the truth. Lying about something is a bad thing and you're a good boy...now go to the shed and get a shovel and we'll bury this poor old dead hen."

I never lied to her again.

Now that I've read Granddaddy's journal I wonder how it made her feel to live the lie about who he really was all those years. I know she did it to protect him, which makes me wonder if that was her reason for trying to burn his sea chest. Was she still trying to protect him? Or could it have been an expression of resentment for his self-absorption with the past, rather than with her, during the final years of their life? Or did her anger flare again when she read his references of affairs with other women? Was destroying what he had written her way of striking him one last time? Or was she afraid that what he had written would cause us to think badly of him; or even that it would bring pain to the Taggert grandchildren who are good and respected people in Franklin County? All this is speculation; we'll never know why.

* * * * *

I could see Granddaddy wasn't well that last summer. His clothes hung loosely on him. He was slow and cautious when he was walking. He'd started using a cane whenever he was away from the house. Sometimes his mouth hung open. His right hand shook badly when he lit a match. At times he would sit on the porch looking down the valley as though we weren't there; even when I was sitting cross-legged at his feet and Grandmother was sitting close to him peeling potatoes or stringing beans, we might as well have been a thousand miles away.

Then, one day when just the two of us were at the pond and I was fishing, he said something that frightened me.

"Listen!" he said.

I kept fishing and listened but heard nothing.

"There it is again...did you hear it?"

"No, sir." I looked at him. He was looking at something across the pond but I couldn't tell what it was.

"It's a heron. Can't you hear it?"

"No, sir."

"Damnit, Lafe, listen!"

That scared me as I had never heard him curse, and I had never heard the name Lafe. "Granddaddy...who's Lafe?"

"What?"

"Who's Lafe?"

He turned and stared at my face. He frowned but didn't answer.

"Granddaddy, I'm George Edward."

He continued to stare for a moment then shook his head, "O yes...I see you. Help me up...I want to go to the house now."

He seemed better the next morning. A little while after breakfast he came around the side of the house to the flower garden where Grandmother and I were weeding. He said he was going to see how the Garners were doing cutting the hay and that he wouldn't be gone long. He had his cane and Shep with him. I looked up once as they went through the gate to the hay field.

Toward noon, when the sun was almost straight up and he had not come back, Grandmother told me to go find him, to see how he was doing and to take him some water and lunch. She filled a fruit jar with water and put it and two sandwiches in a pail.

"George Edward, take this out to him; he'll be under that tree. You be sure now that he drinks some water and eats one of the sandwiches, and after you all are done eating bring him on back with you."

It was blazing hot. The heat rippled the air. At the far end of the field, a mirage shimmered like a lake. The Garners had cut the field the day before and the sweet smell of new-mown hay filled the air. The hay lay in long regular swaths that stretched from the start of the field near the barn lot up the valley to the north end where the woods and the first slope of the mountains began. Meadowlarks and field sparrows were still feeding on the fresh seeds and insects flushed out by the mowing of the hay.

He was where she said he would be, sitting with his back against the trunk of the tree, smoking his pipe. He watched me as I walked across the field through the bright sunlight into the shadow of the giant tree. "I'm glad you've come," he said. He patted the ground beside him. "Sit here."

Shep lay on the other side of him, his grizzled head on my grandfather's leg; my grandfather's hand rested on Shep's back, his fingers gently stroking the black hair. The old dog's eyes were blinking, half closed, almost asleep.
It is interesting to note that a week after my grandfather died, Shep died on the porch beside the door and was buried at the foot of Granddaddy's grave.

I put the lunch pail down in front of him, got the water jar out, handed it to him and sat down. "She told me to tell you to drink it up good and to eat somethin."

He took the jar from my hand, unscrewed the lid, lifted the jar to his lips, took one sip, put the lid back on and handed it to me. I put the jar back in the pail, got a sandwich out and handed it to him. He tore it in two, fed half to Shep and gave the other half to me. Then he took a twist of tobacco out of the side pocket of his overalls, got his knife out and cut off a plug, packed it into the bowl, lit it, took several puffs, slowly turned and looked up the field toward the woods.

Crows were streaming from the trees toward the field; the first ones flew out one at a time and behind them came small bunches. They flew in a straight line from the far end to the field where they dropped down into the mirage. Against the sun's glare, I squinted to see them. They lit all across the shimmering lake; they seemed to be walking on water.

As I watched, I suddenly felt Granddaddy's hand on mine. Then he began to talk and talk and talk....

"George Edward, I want to tell you a story...
about a river...
and a heron...
and a boy...."

Appendix I

[Goodspeed's *History of Tennessee*, 1887]

Franklin County is bounded on the north by Coffee County, northeast by Grundy, east by Marion, south by the State of Alabama, west by Lincoln, northwest by Moore, and contains about 500 square miles, one-fourth of which lies on the Cumberland Mountain and its western escarpment.

The topography of the county is greatly diversified, a portion of it lying on the Cumberland Plateau, a portion in the valley of Elk River, a portion lying on the Highland Rim and a very small portion in the Central Basin...The rim is about 1,000 feet above the level of the sea; the table-land about 2,000, and the basin about 700.

The mean annual temperature of the table-land is 54, of the rim 57, of the basin 58. The soil of the Cumberland Table-land is thin and sterile, but well adapted, on account of its climatic advantages, to the raising of all kinds of fruit. Along the western base of the mountain is a wide belt of land with a dark clay surface and red clay subsoil, furnishing a fine agricultural land. Then come the valley lands of the Elk River, which flows through the county from northeast to southwest. West of the river lie the barrens, so-called, which afford considerable pasture, but the soil is thin and not good for agriculture. In the western portion of the county, and running down the river, is found the black shale formation with its 'rock houses,' or alum and copperas caves, in which are found native alum and copperas.

There are several coves, among which are Farmers' Cove, Lost Cove, Round Cove, and Sinking Cove that lie upon the table-lands, and are wholly shut in by the mountains, beneath which their waters find outlet. Buncombe Cove lies along the base of the mountain and is almost shut in by an outlier. It is watered by the head waters of Bean Creek. There are several other coves, among which is Roark's, one of the largest in the county. The most fertile lands are found in these coves and in the valleys of the Elk and its tributaries. The best timber is found on the mountain slopes, and consists principally of oak, ash, chestnut, beech, poplar, cherry and walnut. The barrens are covered mostly with a light growth of scrubby oak. The Elk River and its tributaries furnish the principal drainage of the county. Mineral springs are abundant, the most noted of which are Hurricane Spring, Estill Springs and Winchester Springs. The former of these springs is a noted summer resort, where thousands of pleasure-seekers make their annual visits. There are also many noted cave springs which furnish pure free-stone water.

There is an extensive marble bed upon Elk River, commencing about five miles below Winchester, and extending down the river ten miles and five miles on either side. The marble is of excellent quality and consists of gray and red, clouded with green porphyry and various shades. This vast mine of wealth had only been slightly developed. Coal has found to exist in great quantities near University place, and at Anderson, Keith's Spring, Maxwell and other points, but, as yet, it has not been mined to any considerable extent.

Many beautiful cascades and waterfalls and caves are found upon the mountains. Natural scenery in the county is extensive. Viewing the mountains from Winchester, their grandeur arises to sublimity. And standing on the mountains and overlooking the valleys of the Elk and its tributaries, with Winchester and its church spires in the foreground, one is led to explain with the poet:

"God hath a being true,
And that ye may see
In the fold of the flower,
The leaf of the tree;
In the wave of the ocean,
The furrow of the land;
In the mountain of granite,
The atom of sand!
Ye may turn your face
From the sky to the sod,
And where can ye gaze
That ye see not a God?"

The settlement of the territory now composing Franklin County began with the beginning of the present century, when all was a vast wilderness, inhabited only by Indians and wild animals. It was a hazardous undertaking to come here in that day and open up a new country west of the mountains where the light of civilization had never shone, and where neither schools, churches, mills, factories, nor any conveniences existed, such as the pioneers had been accustomed to. None but brave and courageous men and women could ever have accomplished such a dangerous and hazardous undertaking....

Appendix II

[The *Memoirs of Lieut. Henry Timberlake, (Who accompanied the Three Cherokee Indians to England in the Year 1762)* was first published in 1765. The following extracts, taken from his journal, describe the appearance and behavior of the Cherokee only a few years before Levi Pearson lived among them for short periods. G. S.]

The Cherokee are of middle stature, of an olive colour, tho' generally painted, and their skins stained with gun-powder, pricked into it in very pretty figures. The hair of their head is shaved, tho' many of the old people have it plucked out by the roots, except for a patch on the hinder part of the head, about twice the bigness of a crown-piece, which is ornamented with beads, feathers, wampum, stained deer hair, and such like baubles. The ears are slit and stretched to an enormous size, putting the person who undergoes the operation to incredible pain, being unable to lie on either side for near forty days. To remedy this, they generally slit but one at a time; so soon as the patient can bear it, they are wound round with wire to expand them, and are adorned with silver pendants and rings, which they likewise wear at the nose. This custom does not belong originally to the Cherokees, but taken by them from the Shawnees, or other northern nations.

They that can afford it wear a collar of wampum, which are beads cut out of clamshells, a silver breast-plate, and bracelets on their arms and wrists of the same metal, a bit of cloth over their private parts, a shirt of the English make. A sort of cloth-boots, and mockasons which are shoes of a make peculiar to the Americans, ornamented with porcupine quills; a large mantel or match coat thrown over all compleats their dress at home; but when they go to war they leave their trinkets behind, and the mere necessaries serve them.

The women wear the hair on their head, which is so long that it generally reaches to the middle of their legs, and sometimes to the ground, club'd, and ornamented with ribbons of various colours, but, except their eyebrows, pluck it from all the other parts of the body, especially the looser part of the sex. The rest of their dress is now become very much like the European; and, indeed, that of the men is greatly altered. The old people still remember and praise the ancient days, before they were acquainted with the whites, when they had but little dress, except a bit of skin around their middles, mockasons, a mantel of buffalo skin for the winter, and a lighter one of feathers for the summer. The women, particularly the half-breed, are remarkably well featured; and both men and women are streight and well-built, with small hands and feet.

The warlike arms used by the Cherokee are guns, bows and arrows, darts, scalping-knives, and tomahawks, which are hatchets; the hammer-part of which being made hollow, and a small hole from thence along the shank, terminated by a small brass-tube for the mouth, makes a compleat pipe...This is one of their most useful pieces of field-furniture, serving all the offices of hatchet, pipe, and sword; neither are the Indians less expert at throwing it than using it near, but will kill at a considerable distance.

They are of a very gentle and amicable disposition to those they think their friends, but as implacable in their enmity, their revenge only being compleated in the entire destruction of their enemies. They were pretty hospitable to all white strangers, till the Europeans encouraged them to scalp; but the great reward offered has led them often since to commit as great barbarities on us, as they formerly only treated their most inveterate enemies with. They are very hardy, bearing heat, cold, hunger and thirst in a suprizing manner; and yet no people are given to more excess in eating and drinking, when it is conveniently in their power; the follies, nay mischief, they commit when inebriated, are entirely laid to the liquor; and no one will revenge any injury (murder excepted) received who is no more himself; they are not less addicted to gaming than drinking, and will even lose the shirt off their back, rather than give over play, when luck runs against them.

They are extremely proud, despising the lower class of Europeans; and in some athletick diversions I once was present at, they refused to match or hold conference with any but officers...

They seldom turn their eyes on the person they speak of, or address themselves to, and are always suspicious when people's eyes are fixed on them. They speak so low, except in council, that they are often obliged to repeat what they were saying; yet should a person talk to any of them above their common pitch, they would immediately ask him, if he thought they were deaf...

As to religion, every one is at liberty to think for himself; whence flows a diversity of opinions among those that do think, but the major part do not give themselves that trouble. They generally concur, however in the belief of one superior Being, who made them, and governs all things, and are never discontent at any misfortune, because they say, the Man above would have it so. They believe in a reward and punishment. After this I need not say that in every particular they are extremely superstitious, that and ignorance going always hand in hand...They seldom bury their dead, but throw them into the river...

* * * * *

These are the stories of my people.

George Spain, 2013
Nashville, Tennessee

CPSIA information can be obtained at www.ICGtesting.com
Printed in the USA
LVOW11*1021211013

357867LV00002B/3/P